kiss me goodnight

jennifer rebecca

Kiss Me Goodnight

Copyright © 2018 Jennifer Rebecca

Cover Design and Formatting by
Alyssa Garcia at Uplifting Designs
Editing by
Stephanie Atienza at Uplifting Designs
www.uplifting-designs.com

ISBN: 978-1-7320747-6-7

For more information about Jennifer Rebecca & her books, visit
www.jenniferrebeccaauthor.com

For Sean

*Thank you for being my very on HEA. a thousand
years with you won't ever be enough.
It was only every you.*

kiss
me
goodnight

*"I was a boat stuck in a bottle,
Never got the chance to touch the sea.
Just forgot on the shelf,
No Wind in the sails,
Going nowhere with no one but me.
I was one in one-hundred billion.
A burned out star in a galaxy.
Just lost in the sky wondering why
Everyone else shines out but me.
But I came alive when I first kissed you,
The best me has his arms around you.
You make me better than I was before.
Thank God I'm yours."*

-Russell Dickerson

prologue

it's you

THERE IS A MARCHING band pounding away in my brain.

I must have had too much to drink at the rehearsal dinner last night. I think. I have to get my ass ready for today—my wedding day—because if I don't, my bestie, Emma, will have my ass.

I pry my eyes open, only then do I realize that I am not in our hotel room on the coast. I'm not in the luxury king sized bed full of fluffy euro pillows and down comforters near a window looking out at the Atlantic Ocean. I'm not where I should be. It takes my brain a minute, still feeling as fuzzy as it is, to realize that I'm not . . . *safe*.

The light shines through the wooden slats of the closet doors just the way that it is in my dreams.

I'm here. Right back where I started. Where I thought I would die when I was so small. Just a baby really. Where I once escaped and had naively thought I would never be back. I scoot back on the worn, torn carpet floor of the closet that I was locked in once before, until my back hits the wall. I try to make myself as small as possible hoping against all hope that he won't see me. But as I hear the footsteps growing louder and louder, I know that there is no hope to be found. No hope at all.

The closet door swings open and I realize how stupid I have been. All this time that I struggled, that I suffered from those terrible nightmares and prayed that they would either end or I would finally remember who had tried to harm me when I was just six years old. All those times I thought I was safe, that I was free, were really nothing but lies because looking down at me with a sinister smile on his face in this little house of horrors from my haunted past is the last person I ever would have thought would be capable of this kind of thing.

I was never free, I was living under the watchful eye of a monster, a wolf in sheep's clothing just waiting for their chance to pounce. His smile broadens and his eyes glimmer with excitement in the knowledge that he's won. It's finally over. This game of cat and mouse that we have been silently engaged in for twenty-four years is ending.

He pulls his leather belt free from his pants and loops it around my neck. I look up into his warm eyes, ones that I had always trusted as he tightens the leather around my neck.

"It's you. It was always you," I say as suddenly every memory finally clicks into place. Anna would be so proud.

I gasp as the air is squeezed out of my lungs.

I struggle to pull more in even though in my brain I know that it isn't possible. Maybe this is how it was always supposed to be. Maybe this is how my story was always supposed to end. My name is Detective Claire Goodnite and I'm about to die.

You know what they say, every story has its ending, I just wish I was prepared for this one.

I can already tell that this one's gonna sting . . .

chapter 1

shots fired

One week earlier . . .

MY ENGAGEMENT RING glitters in the late afternoon sunlight as my hand sits on top of the steering wheel. I had just wrapped up support interviews to help out a fellow detective with their case. There seems to finally be a lull in the excitement here in George Washington Township and I, for one, am glad for it.

Truthfully, after this year, I'm not sure I could handle anymore excitement. One more surprise and the men with the big butterfly nets and funny jackets might come and take me away (ha ha!) to the padded rooms with full service horse tranquilizers.

It's time for my own *Happily Ever After* and I am going to take it.

I have no active cases as Wes and I are getting married in a handful of days. The hall down at the shore has been booked and paid for. It didn't feel right to get married in the church where Anna died. She had thought a beach wedding where bridesmaids wore frothy, light pink dresses sounded delicious and, in her honor, that is exactly what we'll have. Down to the letter. Wes and I are going to make Anna's dream wedding come true. It feels like the perfect way to honor her and her sacrifice. A sacrifice that I still don't fully understand. Thankfully, Wes agrees.

We are getting married for us. This is our time, finally! But the way in which we're doing the deed is all class and romance, it's all Anna.

I can't help the burn in my heart when I think about Anna.

It's been months since she died, and I still cry every night. Luckily, Wes is there to hold me through the night, through it all. Emma hasn't been the same either. I know that she blames herself for what happened but while she didn't make the best decisions, she didn't send Anna careening toward her gruesome end at that church. That rests solely on Anna's shoulders. Well, hers and the sick bastard who murdered her.

Emma blames Lee too.

My poor brother has been struggling to find an inroad with Emma but she isn't budging an inch. He is so desperate to make any progress with her that it's becoming painful to watch him crash and burn every day. I have to wonder, will there come a day when he gives up on her and moves on? If so, will Emma regret it when he does?

I just don't know.

I turn left past the old church on my way back to the station. The ticking of my turn signal beats as fast as my heart when I see the steeple. My palms sweat, and my stomach turns. The new department shrink told me this kind of reaction is normal after a traumatic event. I told him to fuck off.

So, did Emma and Lee.

It's not his fault. I know that and the shrink, if he's worth his salt, probably does too. I let one department shrink into my life five years ago in order to make detective and to be totally honest, after everything that happened to Anna, I just don't have it in me to let anyone else in. It hurts too much when they go.

It was one of my brother Lee's edicts before I could sit the exam. Lee is the Captain of our humble little department which is all well and good when he's kicking crime's ass and taking names. Not so great when he's threatening to fire me every other day. And because he is both my brother and my boss he was well aware that I was kidnapped from our family home when I was six years old. Lee felt that I might have spectacular amounts of baggage—and I do—that might keep me from doing my job. It doesn't but he had no way of knowing.

Lee made me start seeing Anna—only back then she was Dr. Garner—for weekly sessions. I had no way of knowing that she would become family, the sister I never knew that I needed, my ride or die chick, my best friend for life, well at least for the duration of *her life*. That is until she fell in love with my brother, *Deputy Dipshit* as I like to call him, and he fell in love with someone else. It damn near killed Anna. Then, when she decided that she had to prove her worth in our little law enforcement community, to Lee and to everyone else, it finally did kill her when she crossed paths with a psycho.

When I was up for detective, Lee was sure that I would never pass the psych eval. because of my personal history. It's nice to know that he had the utmost confidence in his baby sister and he still does to this day. He made me start sessions with Anna to uncover my past and balance out the heavy shit we have to wade through every day on the job. Somewhere along the way she became my friend.

When I was taken, there were never any ransom demands made, in fact the kidnapper never made contact any with my parents. My dad was the Captain of the department Lee and I work for now. At the time, they had theorized that it had to be someone my dad put away. I can only assume that they intended to never let me go. I guess we'll never really know. And that thought keeps me awake for far more nights than I care to admit.

Fortunately, I was a badass even at six. I broke free and ran away. Unfortunately, I was so malnourished, and sleep deprived that I have little to no memories that include who my attacker was. I know that he was a man, but his face—*or lack thereof*—still haunt me every night. It's like someone took an eraser to his face. I can see so much of the closet where he kept me and the dirty pallet on the floor that was my bed. I hear every heavy footfall of that bastard as he stomped his way to my hiding spot and the way that he would pant a little in excitement when he told me to call him daddy. I can even feel the toes of his boots in my ribs as he kicks me in my dreams. But I can never see his face.

He left me with a handful of memories wrapped up in nightmares that terrorize me every night. Ever since Anna was murdered, I have had several most nights. Starting with one and rolling right into the next and then the next after that until I get out of bed and pace, giving up on peace and a sound night's sleep. It's getting to the point that I'm afraid to fall asleep at night. Worst of all, Wes is starting to notice how bad it's getting. I can't deny it any longer and truthfully, I don't want to. It's time to let Wes in.

But what haunts me the most, is never knowing who he was. I can only assume that to this day, he is still living free. There is even a chance that I know him in some capacity. Maybe he's the guy who delivers my mail or the man who changes the oil in my car.

Maybe I will never know . . .

I sight my scope taking the wind speed and direction into account like any marksmen worth his salt would.

This is really is the perfect spot.

There are fat, greedy businessmen meeting over lunch in a restaurant across the way. It looks like most of them are drinking their lunch. From here I can see people out enjoying their sunny afternoon in the Indian Summer sunshine. A mother with a baby carriage . . . But the icing on the cake is the school group on a field trip to the museum.

Soon they will all learn that no one is safe from me. I am not a man to be messed with! Soon they will all learn that they cannot play games with me because I am the game maker.

"Ahh . . . and there is the man of the hour," I say to myself as a police officer walks around the corner.

I fire the first round into the crowd and watch as they scream and scurry like ants out of an ant hill. I laugh silently to myself as they look around to see where the shots are coming from—but I have chosen this spot perfectly after hours of meticulous consideration.

This is the perfect blind.

I fire another shot and then another.

"There you are, my queen," I coo when I finally see my prize in the crowd.

I knew that she couldn't help herself, she would have to be here at a scene like this. We're not very different here and I. She is the prey and I am the hunter. We are two sides of the same coin really. A Yin and a Yang. She doesn't know it yet, but we belong together.

I watch her move trying to protect the people, she thinks that she is so good. But really, this is all her fault. This blood shed is on her hands. And soon she will learn the hardest lesson of all, that I always win.

And then I set my sights on the male police officer and pull the trigger . . .

My radio crackles to life . . .

"Code 30! Code 30!" It's not every day that an

emergency call for assistance comes over the radio like that and my heart starts pumping.

I pick up the radio and click the button. "This is Detective Goodnite, what is your position?"

"Twenty-third and Main."

"I'm on my way," I reply as I flip on the lights and sirens on my Tahoe.

"Code 30! Code 30! Shots fired . . . officer needs assistance."

"This is dispatch," my radio crackles again. *"All available officers please respond. Be advised this is a hot scene."*

"Officer is advised," I respond.

"Oh Jesus . . . he's shooting at us! He's just shooting everywhere at everyone. It's madness!"

I recognize that voice over the radio. It's Officer Rodriguez. I've known him for years and our cases intersect often as he's out of the same station. He has a wife named Alma and a little girl named Angelina. He told me three weeks ago that Alma is expecting again when he RSVP'd to my wedding.

My stomach somersaults over and over and I'm sure that I might puke. My hands are sweating on the steering wheel. I remind myself that this is nothing like Anna. Everything is going to be just fine. But when I park my car a block over from the scene, nothing is fine.

A sniper is on top of one of the buildings raining open fire on absolutely anyone who happens to be down below. It's insanity and I have never seen anything like it. It only takes me a second to know that the bad man of my past will have some competition in my nightmares tonight.

I unsnap the strap on my holster, pull my sidearm free, and hug the walls of the buildings taking cover where I can as I weave my way over to the scene.

There are civilians everywhere just trying to get out. I have to stop and take a deep breath to focus on anything. Once again, I rely on the SEAL breathing exercise my brother had taught me long ago. I breathe in deeply, holding it there, only to take in even more air, and then one more time. When I meditate at home, I imagine and a three-story building and filling that building up with air one floor at a time before slowly emptying the building but there is no time for that here.

When I slowly expel the air from my lungs, my focus snaps into place just as I was trained to do. I see a young mother with a baby in her arms. She's pinned against the side of the building. Her baby stroller sits abandoned and over turned on the curb not far from where she's hiding now. All of her baby items are spilled out of the discarded bag.

When I look up her eyes so full of fear for her and the tiny pink bundle in her arms hits me full blast. This woman is putting all of her faith in me to get them out of here safely. Without me they wouldn't make it and that is a heavy burden to carry but I will with all of the respect it deserves. "Please help me," she mouths.

I nod to her as I hold up my index finger to my mouth signaling to be quiet. I still don't know where the shooter is, and I don't want her to get caught in the crosshairs on my command.

Other officers and detectives are arriving on the scene. People are running everywhere. It's pandemonium.

There seems to be a lull in the gunfire. I can only hope that the shooter is out of ammunition and they either have no more or need time to reload. Either way, this woman and I aren't going to stick around to find out. I have to get her and her baby out.

I see Jones across the way and I motion to him that I'm going to get these two out of here. He nods that he understands. I make my way over to her and push them towards the wall as I keep my back to her.

"Hold on to my belt," I instruct her. "We're getting you out of here."

"Thank you," she whispers.

I start to move them along the wall using my body to shield them. I'm determined that they get out of here as quickly as possible, so I can get back in there and help more people. But right now, this little baby and her mom are my number one priority.

A quick look around me shows that other officers—some I know and some I don't recognize—are involved in similar tasks. Jones has a couple of frustrated business men and Rodriguez has kids from a school group that was just leaving the museum a couple of doors down.

And then everything happens all at once . . .

The gunfire resumes—I can't see from where—but I pause in my shuffling of the young mother and her baby down the side of the building to try and decipher. No luck. I have to keep moving them. I look at her pale face from over my shoulder.

"You do exactly as I say," I command her in a harsh whisper. "No matter what."

"Okay." I can hear in her voice that she is holding in a sob. This woman is a tough one, but any normal human being would be scared in this situation.

"You stay low and as close to the wall as possible," I order her.

"Okay," she whispers.

"Stay behind me if you can. If something happens to me you keep moving. Stay low, move fast, and watch your surroundings. Do you understand me?" I ask her. I need to hear this woman agree to follow my directions. This is the only way that I can ensure her safety to the best of my abilities.

"Yes," she agrees.

"There are police officers and paramedics waiting just past the building after this one. We just have to get there," I tell her.

"Okay." I can see her nod her head out of my peripheral.

"Just get there," I demand.

I pick up the pace when I notice one of the businessmen, who looks like they had most likely drank their lunch in their afternoon meetings, take a swing at Jones. God dammit! Why can't they just let us evacuate them to safety? Frustration burns in my gut because I know that I can't stop to help him. I have to get this woman and her baby out of here. Fucking assholes.

Jones slugs the businessman, laying him out flat. He catches the drunk ass and throws him over his shoulder in a fireman hold. The rest of the party follow without so much as a snide remark or eye roll as Jones leads them down a different alley than I'm pushing the mom and her baby down. Good for Jones. If he gets reprimanded over that move, I'll make sure to go to bat for him. I heard he's sitting for the Detective's Exam next month and I don't want to see anything get in the way of that. Jones is going to be a damn good detective.

"Keep moving," I say just under my breath. "It's just a little bit further. We just have to keep moving."

I hear the report of the rifle just before a wild shot hits the brick above my head raining chunks of brick and mortar down on us. A sharp piece must have hit me on the forehead by my hairline because I feel a sharp stinging sensation before blood trickles down my face and into my eye and mouth.

The young mother lets out a little scream.

"Hush, we just have to keep moving," I demand. She doesn't answer but just nods as I keep pushing her down the wall.

If she alerts the shooter to our position we are nothing but sitting ducks and I can't let that happen. If anyone is getting out of here alive, it's this woman and her baby. I'll see to it myself if it's the last thing I do, I just hope it's not.

We're almost there when a child's scream rings out. I look back just in time to see Rodriguez, who was corralling the school group from the museum look up at me. He's bleeding from his shoulder and his eyes are wide with fear. No. No no no no no no. No fucking way. I know the look on his face. He knows that he's done. I have seen this look one too many times and I don't want to see it now. I shake my head no.

"Keep moving," I mouth to him.

Rodriguez doesn't acknowledge that I have spoken to him. He just stands there frozen and opens his mouth. When he speaks his voice sends chills down my spine with one word.

"Run."

And then a bullet from some rooftop around us pierces right through his heart cutting his life short.

"Move!" I shout to the mom.

Jones turns around and starts running towards the kids corralling them against the building. I push her faster down the wall. The sooner that I can deposit her with the paramedics, the fast I can get back here to cover Jones and anyone else who may have shown up. I feel so torn. I want to cry over my friend. I want to help Jones get all those kids out and I want to find that fucking shooter. But I can't because I will not abandon this one woman and her child when we're so close to safety.

"Keep going," I order again.

"Okay," she whimpers.

"We're almost there. I can see the end of the building," I tell her. "There's going to be a break in the coverage where we are out in the open. Do not look back, just run for the police blockade. I'll be right behind you."

"But—" she starts. She is going to panic. I can see it in her eyes and I can't let that happen. If she loses it now, this woman won't make it out of here alive.

"No matter what," I reassure her. "I'll be right behind you."

"Okay," she whispers.

"Here it comes," I tell her. "On three, two, one, go!"

We take off. She clutches her baby girl tightly in her arms as she runs for the police blockade. An officer that I don't recognize sees us and motions for us to run in like a third base coach telling his batter to run home. "Go! Go! Go!"

She just passes through the blockade when another shot rings out. It feels like a linebacker hits me from behind and I stumble. No, scratch that. It feels like I'm being run over by an African elephant. I'm pretty sure those are the bigger ones. Although I don't know for sure, and I really don't care right now.

The impact lifts me from my feet for a second and it's like I'm running through the air. Maybe it's the blood loss, maybe it's the hit to the head that I took, but for a second, my mind flashes that I'm just like Michael Jordan in Space Jam. I don't even know if that's who was in that movie, but it seems right. And then my toes touch the ground again and I keep going.

I don't lose my footing even though I stumble. The blood from my forehead is still stinging my eye and blurring my vision.

I just make it through the blockade when my feet stop working. My brain feels like it's full of cotton and everything feels so cold even though it's a warm fall—an Indian summer.

"Detective Goodnite!" someone shouts but I'm not sure who or from where because the edges of my vision are creeping in.

"We made it," I say just before everything goes black.

chapter 2

stitches

LIGHTS. THE LIGHTS ARE so bright.

I blink my eyes open against the rows and rows of large, round spot lights overhead. No, not spotlights, surgical lights.

Something jostles me like an earthquake and I groan.

"Well, it looks like Sleeping Beauty is finally ready to join us," someone says from behind me. I look over and there sits one of my favorite paramedics in the area.

"Hey, Bill," I smile weakly at him. "What happened?"

"You got shot," he tells me.

"Ouch," I cringe. "Well, that sucks."

"That it does, my dear. That it does." I roll my eyes and wince. Ouch. That hurt.

"Well, I say it was only a matter of time the way you Goodnites cowboy around," Bill's partner, Dan, says from his spot in front of me in the driver's seat.

"Hard-de-har-har, asshole," I grumble.

"I try," he chuckles.

"Bill?" I ask.

"Yeah, Claire?" he answers me.

"Do I still have my gun?" I ask sweetly.

Bill opens his mouth to answer me, but Dan beats him to the punch. "Per regulations, the sidearm of an unconscious officer is to be removed and stowed in a locked compartment. Then turned over to a high ranking officer in the chain of command," he sites. I let out a frustrated sigh. Damn.

"Can I have it back now?" I ask sweetly.

"Are you going to shoot Dan?" Bill asks me.

"Maybe." I shrug my shoulders.

"Then no!" Dan shouts from the front of the truck.

"You have to give it back eventually!" I snap. I hate being without it. And it's my very favorite one.

"I'll give it to Wes or Lee," he crows. "They're much nicer."

"Were you always this much of a baby?" I ask Dan.

"No!" he shouts.

"Yes!" Bill corrects at the same time. I bark out a laugh that turns into a yelp as a sharp pain rips through my shoulder.

"Ouch!" I shout. "Mother fucker that hurts."

"Sit back." Bill orders. "And no sudden movements. You were shot for fucks sake."

"Fucker," I mumble under my breath.

"What was that?" Bill asks.

"Nothing," I mutter petulantly like a child who was caught being naughty, not that I have any reason to. I was the one who was shot. A little sympathy would be nice but apparently that's not coming.

"Anyways, sit back and relax," Bill says with an evil smile in his voice. "Because you know O'Connell is going to shit kittens when he finds out you were shot."

"Oh shit."

"So true!" Dan cackles. "Hey, I bet he already knows."

"What?" I ask feeling all of the blood drain from my face.

"It went out over the radio when you were hit," Bill answers.

Shit, shit, shit. I have to call Wes. I have to let him know that I'm alright. I bite my lip and fight past the pain searing through my shoulder as I reach for my jeans pockets only to come up empty.

"Where's my phone?" I demand.

"I have no idea," Bill shrugs. "You must have dropped it somewhere out there."

"Fantastic," I say just as the ambulance pulls to a stop at the Emergency Room entrance to the hospital where I seem to have spent so much of my time over the last year.

"Well, this is where your ride ends," Bill says as Dan pops open the back doors and they unload the gurney that I am strapped to, bouncing me as much as possible. I grit my teeth to keep from crying or screaming or both.

I just know that those assholes are doing it on purpose.

The glass doors of the Emergency Room slide open and a triage nurse runs up to us. Her eyes go wide when she realizes it's me.

"Hey, Josie," I greet her.

"Are you fucking kidding me?" Josie snaps.

"Was it something I said?"

"I don't know what's going to be worse," she answers. "Your man up in here tearing the place apart to get to you or your nut-bag family tearing this place apart to get to you."

"I'm sorry?" I shrug sheepishly.

"Just do me a favor."

"What's that, Josie?" I ask.

"Next time you get hurt do it in another hospital's zone and not mine." The snickers and cackles of both Dan and Bill can be heard throughout the hospital. I shot them both a withering glare but it's Josie who gets those two apes to stop.

"What do we have?" she asks them as they hand of their clipboard for discharge.

"GSW to the upper left shoulder," Bill says.

"Through and through?" Josie asks.

"Looks to be a deep graze," Dan answers.

"And a head trauma and laceration," Bill finishes.

"Well, aren't you just a fun bag of tricks today?" she asks as she looks me over.

"I do like to keep things interesting," I droll. I try to look at my fingernails casually, but it turns awkward when I realize that my arms are strapped into the gurney. I let out a heavy sigh.

"Take her to bay five," Josie orders.

The boys wheel me through the open corridor of the ER, past the central nurse's station, and through the drab blue curtain of what I can only assume is bay five. Fantastic.

"On three," Bill says.

"Wait, guys—" I start but they don't listen as they unbuckle the straps of the gurney and the blood begins to flow back to my uninjured arm.

"One . . ." I try to scramble to get my bearings but with one arm I am fairly unbalanced. "Two . . ."

"Guys, really," I plead.

"Three . . ." And then they hoist me up and onto the bed in bay five. Even though I knew it was coming, it still catches me by surprise and I let out an undignified squeak which I know will be making the rounds of the station by the time I get back there because both Bill and Dan don't even bother to hide their mirth at my expense.

My cell phone falls out of my pocket as they move me, and I fall on it like an alcoholic falls onto a bottle they forgot they had. Thank God! I need to call Wes and tell him that I'm alright, so he doesn't freak out but when I hit the home button the screen won't light up. The battery is dead as a doornail. Fuck!

"Goddamnit," I gripe.

"Don't laugh," Josie says as she makes her way into the bay. "You all are just as bad patients as she is. It's a hazard of the trade, I guess."

"Not true," Dan gripes.

"So true. Now get out," she commands with a smile on her face.

"We're not back in service until we can release her firearm to her department lead," Bill says with a wicked smirk.

"You could just release it back to me," I tell them.

"That's not true and you know it," Josie reprimands

me.

"I know but it was worth a try."

"Not in my hospital it's not."

"Ugh, fine," I concede.

"Now, you two out of the bay so the doctor can get in here and stitch her pretty ass back up," Josie says as she shoos them out just in time for a tall woman with brown hair twisted up into a bun with streaks of silver shot through it. She's beautiful.

"Hello, I'm Dr. Emory," she tells me with a smile on her face. "You must be Detective Goodnite. I've heard so much about you."

"Call me Claire," I tell her.

"Claire it is," she says before turning to Josie. "What do we have here?"

"GSW in the upper left shoulder, a head wound, and laceration," Josie answers.

"Let's irrigate the wound and see what we have," the doctor tells Josie as she snaps on a pair of latex gloves after scrubbing her hands in the sink.

The doctor peels away the bandage on my forehead and begins cleaning it.

"What happened here?" she asks me.

"Sniper shot the brick wall behind me and I got hit with a chunk. It's not so bad," I answer.

"I heard about the sniper on the radio," she says.

"Yep," I answer because I can't talk about it until I have been debriefed.

"It appears that it isn't that bad. Head wounds tend to bleed a lot though," she says thoughtfully as she tends to the wound. "I don't think it need stitches."

"Fantastic." The doctor places steri-strips on my

forehead before covering it with a clean bandage.

"I can't say the same for the shoulder though," she tells me as she moves on and undresses the bandage that Bill put on to stop the bleeding in the truck.

"Damn."

"Yeah," she says. "By the look of it, you're lucky it was just a graze. Anything lower and you'd probably be dead." As the words are coming out of her mouth my blood runs cold. It could happen to anyone of us on any day. But today I was on a bullshit assignment and never thought the day would end like this. A day where I watched another friend die right before my eyes.

"This is probably going to sting a little," the doctor says as she injects something to numb the pain while she stitches me back up.

"Yeah," I answer a little lost in my own thoughts. "It already does."

"I'll be as quick as I can." And she does. I have never had a doctor stitch me up as fast as she does before placing another bandage over her handiwork to keep it clean.

"Thanks," I say.

"Don't thank me yet," she says shining a small flashlight in my eyes. "I'd say you have a mild concussion and need rest. The nurse is going to give you an antibiotic injection to stave off infection and those hurt like a bitch." I can't help but laugh at her cursing. She was all prim, proper, and class right up until now.

"Okay," I laugh until Josie hits me with the mother of all shots that does, in fact, burn like a bitch but was nothing in comparison to actually being shot. "Argh! Shit shit shit!"

"I told you," the nurse says.

The doctor opens her mouth to say something to me but then a commotion breaks out in the ER just outside those ugly blue curtains.

"I knew I should have bet money on your man," Josie says.

"Oh shit," I mumble as the curtain is roughly shoved back and Wes, with a wild look in his eyes steps into the bay.

"'Oh shit' is right," the doctor mumbles. "I'll just get your discharge orders ready."

"I'm gonna fucking kill you!" he roars as the doctor races around him.

"Not in my hospital you won't because then I'd just have to put her back together again," Josie tells Wes on a raised eyebrow. "You heard me!"

Wes just sighs and rolls his eyes.

"It's not that bad," I defend holding up my good arm before Wes can get a word in. He narrows his eyes. "Well . . . I guess it kind of is. My dress is strapless, and the good doctor tells me this is going to leave a scar."

"That's not fucking funny, Claire!" Wes thunders into the room.

"I'm sorry," I tell him. "You're right it's not funny. I don't have a dress at all yet."

"How could you, Claire?" he asks his voice no eerily calm. It's when he's calm that worries me the most. When his voice is controlled and steady is when Wes is his most emotional.

"I had to help them," I defend myself. He sighs and runs a hand through his hair. "I couldn't just leave those people there. I couldn't just let everyone else work to protect those people while I sat back and took it easy. You know that."

"I know," he tells me. And he does. Wes wouldn't want me to be the kind of person who doesn't stop to help someone in need, but it conflicts with his need to have me safe and accounted for.

"I'm okay," I tell him.

"Okay," he says making his way over to me. I scoot over so that he can sit next to me on the hospital bed and he wraps an arm around me, gently holding me. I can hear Wes's frantic heartbeat under my ear.

"Can I have my gun back?" I ask into the stillness of the room.

"No fucking way," he says quietly into my hair.

I sigh. "I thought as much."

chapter 3

we'll just see about that

"**A**LRIGHT, GIRL, YOU'RE ALL SET," Josie says as she pushes the drab blue curtain aside and walks back into the bay with my discharge papers. "Don't do anything crazy, lots of rest, but not too much rest because of the concussion."

"So, I need to wake her up every hour?" Wes asks with an evil glint in his eyes that I don't quite trust.

"It couldn't hurt, but it's not a bad concussion. She needs to keep her stitches dry and she has a prescription for antibiotics. You can fill it at the pharmacy here or have it filled anywhere else," she explains.

"Thanks," Wes says pocketing the little blue square of paper.

"Well, I'll just leave you guys to it. Here are some spare scrubs and a pair of flip flops from the gift shop so you can leave because, well, you look like total shit and those clothes need to go in the garbage," Josie informs me before turning on her heels and walking out of the bay. Wes doesn't laugh because he's still too mad at me, at the situation, at everything to let himself but the corner of his mouth does lift in an interesting twitch that leaves me hopeful.

"Ready?" he asks me once we are alone.

"Yeah," I answer softly. I know that I scared him. Hell, I scared me too. I think it's best to just let Wes have a little quiet to sort out his thoughts and just maybe I need a moment too.

Carefully, I push up off of the hospital bed and move to stand. I start to try and pull my tattered shirt over my head but even with one shoulder cut away I still can't manage it. I'm sure that a frown mars my face between my brows as I struggle.

Wes steps forward and gently brushes my hand away. He gently pulls my top over my head and then down around my injured arm to avoid jostling it. He scowls when he notices the bandage on my shoulder after he uncovers it. I feel bare—vulnerable—standing in front of him in nothing but my lace bra with all of my wounds exposed.

Wes raises his hand and with a gentle tenderness he brushes back the wisps of hair that fell from my ponytail. What a mess I must look like and yet, when I raise my face to meet his eyes, I see nothing but love and worry. Wes looks at me like I am the most beautiful woman in the world even when I am at my worst and it reminds me that even after one of the worst days imaginable, I have Wes to go home to.

As long as I have Wes, I can survive anything else that comes my way.

Wes places a soft kiss on the top of my head before pulling back just enough to unsnap my jeans and push them down my thighs only to become tangled up in my favorite boots. I let out a heavy sigh. Wes guides me back to sit on the edge of the hospital bed so that he can pull my tall, gray boots from my feet one by one.

"Don't throw those out!" I panic at the thought. I love those damn boots.

Wes smirks. "I wouldn't dare."

"Thank you."

Wes doesn't respond other than a quick nod before pulling my jeans the rest of the way down my legs and then sliding the scrub pants up. He offers me a hand to help me up and I take it placing my good hand in his. Wes pulls me up to stand and then rolls the scrub top in his hands and slides it over my head and my good arm through the arm hole.

"Umm . . ." he hums as he clearly realizes we should have put my injured arm in first. "Let's try that again."

Wes pulls the oversized top back over my head and straightens it out before gingerly guiding my injured arm through the armhole and pulling it over my head, I can then slide my good arm through. Wes pops the tags off the flip flops before dropping to one knee in front of me. Wes slides his hand down my calf before lifting my foot and placing the sandal on it before carefully lowering my foot back to the ground. He repeats the process making me feel a little like Cinderella and not like the walking disaster that I am.

Wes rises to his feet again and turns me around. He gently pulls the rubber band from my hair shaking out my haphazard ponytail and massaging my scalp in the process. I lean back into his hands and let out a little whimper. His hands feel so good and I feel like I was in a car crash. Before I'm ready, Wes pulls his hands from my hair and then quickly plaits my hair in a loose braid. Just the way he did when I was a little girl and when I was last in the hospital.

This tender side of Wes always makes my heart skip a beat.

"Let's go," he says to me as he holds out his hand. I take it without hesitation like always.

Wes scoops up my boots and pockets my dead cell phone before leading me out the door and down the hallway. I smile at Josie as Wes pulls me through the ER and back out of the sliding glass doors. In fact, Wes pulls me through the parking lot and over to his Fedmobile. He beeps the locks on the key fob and drops my hand to pull open the passenger door for me. Once I climb in, he slams my door shut before pulling open the back-passenger door and dumping my boots in the back unceremoniously.

Wes stomps around the hood of the car. He's clearly not over his anger yet. I know that I scared him pretty bad, but still, I was the one that got shot and it's not like I did it on purpose. He's acting like this was my plan all along. Ugh!

I hope he thaws out some on the drive home but as he drives through town it seems that he isn't calming down any. Actually, by the time Wes pulls into the driveway, he seems madder that when he arrived at the hospital in the first place. This doesn't bode well for the rest I'm supposed to be getting.

Wes puts the car in park and turns it off. He steps from the car and slams his door before stomping around to the passenger side before wrenching the door open.

"Wes?" I ask but he just holds out a hand to help me from the car which I take.

He says nothing as he pulls me up the walk to the front door. I stand there in silence and Wes fumes while he unlocks the front door. He pulls me through the threshold before slamming the door shut. The lock sounds like a gunshot in the quiet house and I can't help but jump. It's been a long fucking day and I'm all nerves and frayed edges. My jumpiness seems to make Wes even more angry and he utters an oath under his breath, making me cringe a little.

"Wes?" I ask again but he just takes my hand and leads me through the house.

Wes turns on no lights leaving our space awash in the glow of late afternoon sunset. He leads me up the stairs and down the hall straight to our bedroom. He pushes open the door and I follow him through where he stops and turns to me.

Carefully, Wes slides the scrub top from my body tossing it to the floor. He reaches behind me, unhooking my bra and sliding it from my shoulders—letting my breast hang free. He unties the waistband of the scrub pants and pushes them down my legs, taking my panties with them. I step out of them and my flip flops. Wes thrusts his hands into my braid and drops his forehead to mine leaning to the side, careful of my bandage.

"I can't lose you, Claire," his painful whisper echoes through the late afternoon.

"You're not going to lose me." I place my free hand on his cheek, holding him to me while I reassure my man that I'm here, that I'm alright.

"I can't lose you," he repeats.

"I'm right here, Wes, and I'm just fine."

"You're not fine!"

"It's nothing that a few stitches and some antibiotics can't cure," I tell him, pulling his face down to kiss me.

"We'll see," he pouts before taking over the kiss.

"I'm right here, Wes. Feel me," I plead with him as I grab his hand in mine and place it over my chest so that he can feel the beat of my heart for himself. "Feel me."

The pain in Wes's eyes turns feral.

"I don't want to hurt you."

"Then don't," I push him. "But you should know by now that I'm made of tougher stuff than glass."

"Claire, I don't think—" he starts but I stop him.

"Maybe this is exactly what you need," I tell him. "Maybe this is exactly what I need," I say as I push his hand over a few inches to cover my breast.

He squeezes it gently, letting his thumb glide over my nipple. I wait in unsure silence for him to make his decision, but it's when Wes opens his mouth to give me my answer that I know that I have won this round.

"You better lay down," he orders, and I am happy to comply.

I can't help the smile that plays on my lips as he begins to strip off his suit starting with his tie before unbuttoning his shirt. I watch with rapt attention as piece by piece his clothing hits the floor. This is my Wes. This is us. I knew he couldn't stay mad for too long. A wicked smirk tugs at the corner of his sexy mouth as he moves the pillows from the head of the bed to the middle motioning for me to lay down crosswise with my legs hanging off the side of the bed.

"You think you won this round, don't you?" he asks me as I settle back into the pillows. I look up into his eyes as I answer him.

"Well, yeah." I slow blink. I mean we are naked. So yeah, I did win.

"We'll just see about that," he says as he drops to his knees in front of me and tosses my legs over his shoulders.

Wes does not give me a chance to prepare of catch my breath before sliding his strong hands underneath me, gripping my ass in a firm hold and spreading me open before him. I bite my lip as he licks my pussy completely, rolling his tongue over my clit again and again. Not letting up for even a second. I'll never last like this, but then again, that's exactly what Wes wants.

I thrust my fingers into his hair, holding him tight to me. It's my only anchor in the storm that he's raging over my body between Wes holding my hips down and my injured arm hanging limply at my side.

"Wes," I call out as he gives me no relief from his torture as he hurdles me closer and closer to the edge. "I-I-I'm going to come."

"Let it happen," he rumbles against my core.

Wes continues to suck and bite and lick with the sole purpose to drive me to the brink. I am helpless to do anything but take it and oh how I want to take it. If this is my punishment for scaring the hell out of Wes I will gladly take it with a smile on my face.

"Wes, Wes, Wes," I chant over and over.

I lose my grip on his hair and tear at the bedding underneath me with my good hand. Wes doesn't just eat me, he devours me with abandon and I am lost. My whole body seizes. I close my eyes tight and arch my back as best as I can and come.

Wes releases me from his hold and stands to his full height, towering over me as I lay sprawled on the bed. I feel him line the tip of his cock up with my entrance but still he waits.

"Look at me," he commands. "Open your eyes and look at me."

The second my eyes flutter open and lock with his he thrusts deep letting me take all of him. I feel a twinge in my shoulder but it's so worth it. I school my face as best I can so that he won't notice.

Wes pushes my legs open wide and grips my upper things in his powerful hold as he slowly glides his cock in and out, in and out. From this angle I can see how slick he is from me as he sinks his cock in over and over. It's mesmerizing.

"Wes," I whisper lost in the moment.

"This," he says sliding his fingers through my wetness where his cock joins with my body again and again. "This is all mine. Do you see this?"

"Yes," I breathe.

"This is for me and me alone," Wes tells me something I already know as he thrusts deep inside me.

"Yes," I whisper as he pumps his cock again.

"I'm the one that makes you this wet." He slides out only to drive back in to the hilt.

"Yes, yes, only you," I chant. At this moment I would promise him anything.

"I'm the one that gets to eat this pussy," Wes growls as he powers deep again and again.

"Yes, yes."

"And it's my cock that gets to sink deep inside you," he growls as he does just that again and again, so slowly it's maddening.

"Yes, Wes."

"And it's me who gets to make you come," he says as he circles my opening around his length. "With my mouth, with my fingers, and definitely with my cock."

"Yes," I pant as he moves his thumb to my clit pressing down as he circles in time with his hips.

"Do it now," he commands as he plunges deep. "Come for me."

I call out his name and then I do.

Wes leans over me and drives deep. He pushes my hip down in his hand to meet his hard thrusts which are fast and faster now although he is still careful not to jar my arm. I wrap my good arm around him and hold on tight.

"Again!" he shouts.

"I-I don't know. I don't think I can," I whimper.

"You can," he says as he plunges in over and over again hitting all the right spots.

"Wes," I plead.

"You can!"

And then I do exactly as he says, digging my nails in his back as I do. Wes thrusts once, twice, before roaring his release as he follows me over the edge.

He frames my face in his hands as he slowly glides in and out sending shivers up my spine. I love Wes like this, when he's tender after. He places his forehead to mine and looks deep in my eyes.

"I can't lose you, Claire."

I cover his hand with my own. "You won't lose me."

"I can't, Claire. I won't survive it."

"You won't," I promise him. "For better or worse, I'm right here and I'm not going anywhere."

"You're right here," he repeats my words back to me.

"With you," I promise. "I'm always here with you."

"With me," he repeats.

"I think we're even taking vows proclaiming such in a week." I smile at this man that I love more than anything in this world.

He swats my thigh gently in retaliation. "I'm serious, Claire."

"So am I. I'm fine, Wes," I say pressing my mouth to his.

Wes quickly takes over the kiss obviously needing to reassure himself that I am still here. That I really am just fine. Alive. And it breaks my heart a little that he needs to, but I love him, and I'll give him this moment. Then together, we'll put the pieces back together.

Wes lifts me up in his arms like a bride as he puts the pillows back where they were at the head of the bed and pulls back the covers. He deposits me in the middle like a queen before heading into the bathroom. I hear the water run for a second before he comes back to me carrying a washcloth. I blush as I he tends to me which only makes him roll his eyes and laugh.

"I'll be taking care of you for the rest of my life, beautiful, you might as well get used to it now." He winks at me before heading back into the bathroom.

"And I'll be taking care of you for the rest of mine!" I shout to his retreating back.

"I wouldn't have it any other way," he says softly as he climbs into bed beside me and pulls the covers over us.

Wes wraps himself protectively around me as he drifts off to sleep. I let the soft sound of his even breathing lull me into a gentle sleep that would stay anything but because when I'm asleep, even Wes can't keep the monsters at bay.

chapter 4

familiar

*W*ES AND LIAM ARE *so mean! I can't believe they won't let me hangout with them. I bet they're just afraid that I'll tell mom and Mrs. O'Connell about the magazines they're hiding with the girls in bikinis in them.*

I'm stomping through the woods behind our house. I don't need those gross boys to have some fun. And those boys are gross! They smell weird and put on too much stinky spray stuff when they think I'm not looking.

I just make it to the street on the other side of the trees from our house when a white van pulls up next to me. I hear my mom in my head telling me not to talk to strangers. I feel my eyes going wide as he steps out of the van.

"Claire!" he says, and I wonder how he knows my name. "There you are. I need your help!"

"What do you need help with?" I ask.

"I'm so glad you asked, Claire," he says my name

again like he says it all the time. It's weird but I don't think too much about it. "My puppy, Millie, got out. She's missing. Can you help me find her?"

"I don't know. I should probably go back home . . ." I say.

"No!" he shouts, and it startles me and I jump a little. His eyes widen when he notices my reaction. "I need you to look for her while I drive around. I'll give you this candy bar if you help me . . ." he offers, holding up my most favorite kind. I instantly grab for it, but he pulls it back.

"Okay, what does she look like?" I ask.

He smiles a creepy smile showing all of his teeth, but I open the front door and get in the van. He hands me the candy bar and I realize that I don't even know what his name is . . .

"She's little and fluffy and white . . ." he trails off as I dig into the sweets my mom never lets me eat before dinner. Ever!

All of a sudden, my head feels funny and my ears feel full of cotton like last summer when I got an infection from swimming too much. I open my mouth to tell him something is wrong, but my words don't work. They won't come out! I turn my head to look at him, a scream stuck in my broken mouth. He just smiles his big, creepy smile and everything goes black . . .

When I wake up I'm on an old, yucky blanket on the floor of a dark, smelly house. It's not my house. I know that. I rub the side of my head, it hurts so much. When I look up, the strange man is leaning back in an old torn chair, his feet spread wide and there's a strange bump in the front of his pants that he keeps rubbing his hands on. He smiles when he notices that I'm awake and for the first time ever, I'm scared.

"Hello, Claire, I'm glad that you're awake," he says to me in a scary voice. I just sit there staring with my eyes big. "You may call me daddy."

My breath seizes in my lungs and I wake with a start. I bolt straight up in the bed clutching the sheets and blankets to my chest.

"Claire?" Wes calls from behind me. I can hear the sleep in his voice and know that I woke him from a sound sleep. A deep sleep that he undoubtedly needed.

"Yeah, Wes?"

"Are you okay, honey?" he asks me.

"I'm fine, baby. Go back to sleep," I tell him softly, but he doesn't go back to sleep. Wes sits up in bed behind me curling a long leg up next to me on either side. Wes wraps his arms tight around me from behind.

"Bad dream?" he asks me.

"Yeah," I answer taking a deep breath. There is something about this dream that is bothering me more than they usually do. I just can't put my finger on it.

"You wanna talk about it?" Wes asks and truthfully, I don't . . . but also I do. I know that if I don't share this part of my life—for worse or for better—with Wes I will one day lose him to it. He's either all in or he's out and I am not going to keep secrets from him. I know he's waiting out my silence for an answer . . . for anything really and I'm going to give it to him.

"Actually, I do," I answer as bravely as I can be.

Wes squeezes me briefly before saying, "Tell me what happened."

"It was the day I was taken," I tell him.

"What happened that day?" he asks. I know that he has read the transcripts from after I was found. At first, I was angry with Wes. This was an invasion of my privacy, but the closer we became, I realized how deeply that day affected Wes as well. I'm not the only one who had their life changed forever that day.

I can tell by the way that he leans into me and rubs my shoulder gently that he also wants to know if this was a nightmare or am I actually remembering. For the first time ever after I had a nightmare, I'm actually excited to see how close to the truth my brain is staying.

"I remember . . ." I start. Wes just holds me while he waits for me to collect my thoughts. I feel like it'll feel better to just get it out faster like vomit, it's better not to let it linger, so I open my mouth and let it all spill out in all of its ugly little details. "I remember I was so mad at you and Lee because you wouldn't let me hangout with you. I know now how silly that was."

I feel him tense behind me, but he has to know. Wes has to hear it all.

"I went walking through the woods even though I wasn't supposed to, but I was so mad that I just didn't care—I was so mad that it made me reckless. It's all my fault," I admit my frustration out loud which is something I have never done before.

"Honey, you were just a little girl," Wes says softly.

"I know that, I do, but still, if only I was more careful . . . I don't know . . . something!" I hate how frustrated it makes me. I feel so stupid.

"We can't go back, baby, only forward and we go together," Wes says softly.

I take a deep breath. "I know."

"So, then what happened?" he asks me.

"I guess I had walked farther into the woods than I had realized because when I hit a road I knew I was in trouble."

"What road?" Wes asks me.

"I don't know," I admit. "I know I got there from my house, but I was so mad at you guys that I wasn't paying very good attention."

"That's okay," he reassures me. "We don't need that now. Let's keep going."

"Okay," I agree. I can't go back, only forward.

"What happened next?"

"I realized that I was farther away from home than I had thought I was when I hit the road. I knew I needed to turn around and go back home, but then a man in a white panel van pulled up and asked me for help finding his dog. So stupid, right?"

"Not stupid, Claire, you were just a little girl," he tells me what I already know for the umpteenth time.

"I know, I know." I hold my hands up. I scrub them down my face before pressing on. "I knew I shouldn't go with him, but, Wes?"

"Yeah, baby?"

"He knew my name. He knew who I was when he stopped for me. I-I-I don't think it was random," I tell Wes what I know in my heart.

"I don't think it was random either," Wes agrees.

"Okay." I take a deep breath trying to slow my racing heart.

"Then what happened?" he asks me.

"I climbed into the van and he gave me my favorite candy bar. It was before dinner and everything and I wanted it. So, I unwrapped it and ate it right there in the front seat."

"And then what?" he says softly rubbing my back as he talks me through one of the worst days of my life.

"And then I felt funny. Like my tongue wouldn't work anymore. I felt like I was at the far end of a really long and dark tunnel. And I felt so so sleepy."

"And then what happened, Claire?"

"And then everything goes blank and when I woke up I was in a dirty room on an old blanket. The man was sitting on the sofa . . . he was just sitting there, Wes, watching me."

"What did he do when he noticed you were awake?" Wes asks.

"He told me I could never go home and that I was to call him daddy from now on. That's when I usually wake up." A shudder wracks my body. I hate that part of the dream. I hate how filthy it makes me feel.

"And did you wake up then this time?" he asks me.

"Yeah," I answer.

"What did he look like? Did you recognize him?" Wes asks.

"I can't ever see his face," I explain. "It's just . . . blurry or out of focus. But . . ."

"But what?" Wes asks. He's clearly holding back his frustration that I can't remember. That we both need to know who it is once and for all, so we can lay these demons to rest and move on with our lives.

"But I think something was different this time," I say.

"Like what? What was different?" Wes asks.

"There was something about his voice that sounded almost . . ." I trail off.

"Almost what?" Wes asks hanging onto every word of my description.

"Familiar," I finish. "I think I know whoever took me. Not that I just recognize them, but that they are familiar to me."

"Shit," Wes bites out.

"Yeah," I agree.

"Do you feel a little better?" he asks, and I can hear the hopefulness in his voice.

"Yeah, I do," I answer as I hold onto his arms wrapped around me.

"Wanna try and go back to sleep now?" Wes asks me.

"Yeah, I do."

We lay back down in our bed and Wes pulls me into his arms. I turn at the last second to that I'm face to face with him. I want him to see how much I appreciate him and how much I love him for helping me through this moment.

"When are you going to stop saving me?" I ask him my voice sounding so small.

"Probably never." He shrugs. "I kinda like it. Plus, you've got a great ass."

"I love you, Wesley O'Connell."

"And I love you, Claire."

He pulls his arms tighter around me, grounding me

to the here and now more surely than I could ever have done myself. But even though he makes me feel safe and protected, I hear Anna's voice in my head telling me I need to find out the truth or I will never truly know peace again. And as I drift off to sleep I know that that is exactly what I'm going to do. I will uncover all the secrets of my past even if it kills me. Too bad I would find out later that it probably would.

chapter 5

stay put

BEEP . . . BEEP . . . BEEP . . . Wes uncurls his arm from around me to silence the alarm on his phone that sits on the nightstand. As much as I don't want to leave this bed, I know that we have to face the day. Officer Rodriguez and his wife and child deserve our full attention. The mother and her baby, the school group, even those asshole businessmen deserve to have my full focus on this investigation.

So, it's not really about me and what I want or don't want. It's about settling a score. It's about righting a wrong. I can't bring Rodriguez back, but I can find him justice.

I pull the covers back on my side of the bed and roll over to push myself up to get up out of bed when an arm snakes around my waist from behind, hauling me back into the bed.

"Where do you think that you're going?" Wes asks me, his deep voice gruff with sleep.

"To work?" I ask.

"No," he says with finality. "Try again."

"To the station to catch up on paperwork?"

Wes just shakes his head. "Un-uh. Try again."

"To your office to hang out with you?"

"Absolutely not," he says crossing his arms over his chest.

"Oh, come on!" I shout throwing my hands up in the air. "You have to let me into the bat cave some time." Wes just raises an eyebrow as he stares me down. "Please?"

"No," he says shaking his head. "You, my gorgeous girl, are going to stay put."

"Says who?" I demand.

"Guess."

"You can't make me," I say crossing my own arms across my chest mirroring his stance as I sit in the bed.

"You were shot yesterday, Claire," he says his voice low.

"It was a flesh wound!"

"Claire—"

"I'm fine, Wes!"

"You have a concussion," he tells me something that I already know and that I cannot dispute.

"Sort of . . ." I hedge.

"No, baby, there is no 'sort of' about head trauma."

"I'm—" I start only to be cut off by Wes again.

"Baby, if you say that you are fine one more time I am seriously going to lose it."

"Okay," I say softly.

"Just stay in the bed," he smiles before standing to head to the shower.

"But what if I don't want to?" I ask as he starts to move away from the bed. Wes turns back to look at me with a wicked gleam in his eyes.

"I'll call Lee," Wes volleys back as he turns around and prowls back towards where I'm laying in the bed.

"Lee wants Rodriguez's killer found and bad," I tell him something he already knows is true.

"I'll call your dad," Wes tells me as he sits back down on the edge of the bed next to me. "In fact, that sounds like a great idea . . ."

I shrug as if it doesn't bother me one way or another. "I could always bribe you . . ."

"Ahh, now bribing a Federal Agent is a pretty serious offense," Wes says his voice low and rough. "What did you have in mind, baby?"

And then I lean into him, pressing him back into the bed on his back with my good side before shimmying down his body. I balance myself on my knees between Wes's spread legs and look him directly in the eyes as I lean over and take his hard cock into my mouth.

"That'll do," he says after clearing his throat. "For now."

I widen my stance just a little bit for better balance and tentatively reach for him with my injured arm. It doesn't hurt so wrap my fingers around his base and stroke. Wes groans a little in the back of his throat and he clenches his fists at his sides.

I swirl my tongue around the tip of his cock and lean forward just a little more, bracing myself on his muscular thigh. I bob, sliding my mouth up and down his hard length triggering another growl to escape Wes's sexy mouth.

He squirms on the bed, tipping his hips ever so slightly as if he can't help himself. Wes is barely holding himself back from thrusting up into my waiting mouth. The fact that Wes is so turned on that he can hardly contain himself has my body heating up.

It turns me on that I turn him on.

I clench my thighs together as I swirl my tongue around the tip of his cock again and again. I run them together like a cricket seeking some kind of relief but it's no use. I can't help myself. As I push Wes closer and closer to the edge, I let go of my grip on his thigh and slide my hand down, down, down, to in between my own legs. I slide my fingertips through my own wetness and gasp around Wes's hard length causing it to slide deeper into my mouth. I swirl my finger around my clit faster and faster in time with the way that I slid his cock in and out of my mouth. I'm almost there . . .

"Are you touching yourself?" Wes asks just before he knifes forward to grab me under my arms dislodging him from my lips and pulls me up up up until he can twist at the waist and gently toss me back against the pillows.

"No?" I ask just a little bit breathless.

"I'll ask again," he says looming over me. Wes uses his knee to nudge my legs wider so that he can settle in between my thighs. "Were you touching yourself?"

"Uh huh," I answer honestly with my chin to my chest so that I can look him in the eyes.

And then Wes slides in deep.

"Wes," I breath.

"Maybe." He pulls back and drives in deep. "If I fuck you hard enough, you won't be able to walk."

"Wes." I roll my hips trying to take him deeper.

"Let alone try and leave this fucking house." He plunges in again.

"Yes." I need him so much. I need him hard and deep and fast but he's only giving me so much. Wes is teasing me. And I *just need* so much.

"So, you'll stay put."

"Oh God," I moan as I clench around him.

"That's it, baby," he says as he thrusts again and again.

"Wes," I plead.

"Give it to me," he forces out through his gritted teeth. "It's mine and I want it." And then I do. I throw my head back and scream his name as I come.

I dig my nails into his shoulders and clench my thighs around his hips as he powers deep into my body again and again. I love the way his body moves over and into mine, sweat dripping down his muscular body, one that I am more than happy to get to spend the rest of my life worshipping.

Sex with Wes has never been bad, and it's only gotten better with time. He was good at twenty-six, but he's life changing at thirty-eight. A religious experience between the sheets and a real man that loves me unconditionally during the day. Wes is the whole package and then some.

I feel it building again as Wes drives forward with so much power that the headboard rocks against the wall with the same electric force that he rocks my body and once again, I am powerless to stop it.

I hold him tighter with my whole body, with everything that I have as if I could pull him deeper into me and keep him there. My body is burning with the embers of a fire that only Wes could light and keep burning. He drives forward again, and I am lost to the flames, calling out to him as I come. Wes tips his head back exposing the column of his throat and growls his release as he follows me over the edge.

We lay together for what feels like hours but couldn't be more than a few stolen moments while our breaths even out and the sweat cools. My arm burns like a little bitch, but it was so worth it. Wes kisses the corner of my mouth touching the very tip of his tongue to my lip before taking it away. He leans back to look at me with a smug look on his face that is wholly deserved.

"There," he says as he climbs from the bed. "Now you'll stay put."

"Asshole," I make a half-hearted attempt to shout at him as he saunters off to the shower. I could be pissed at him but . . . well . . . *he's not wrong.*

chapter 6

playing hooky

I LAY BACK LETTING my body sink down into the mattress and take a deep breath. It feels like the down will swallow me up if I let it and I'm half tempted to do just that. Wes was right to be so confident because my entire body is like an over cooked spaghetti noodle.

I feel nothing but the slight burn in my shoulder and the echoes of an ache in my temple. But that's it. Nothing more.

I let myself shut my eyes and just float adrift in my afterglow—not quite asleep but not fully awake either—just letting the early morning sun slither through the curtains and across my skin and over the backs of my eyelids while listening to the birds outside. Something I have never done before. I guess it takes being shot to stop and smell the roses.

I crack an eyelid when I hear footsteps and a swishing sound. Wes is standing there, peeking around the corner from the bathroom with nothing but a towel slung low across his hips. So low that I can see that tantalizing vee that leads down to the promise land.

"Just checking," he mumbles before turning tail and heading back to the closet to dress.

"Just checking what?" I manage to ask but by the time I get the words out of my sleepy mouth, he had already gone so I let myself drift back to my morning catnap among my downy clouds.

I'm not sure how long I had laid there in my absent thoughts when strong hands pull me up and out of my cocoon. I find myself cradled in Wes's muscular arms. He gently crashes his lips to mine and kisses the hell out of me. And I let him. I let his tongue stroke the seam of my lips for entry and I give him that too. But it's doesn't last long. Before I know it, Wes is depositing me back into my fluffy nest and I am powerless to do anything but blink as he kisses my forehead.

"Be good," he orders softly as he walks out the door. I can't help but think how good his ass looks in his Fed suit before I drift back to sleep.

"Come out of the closet, baby."

"No," I whisper, tears hot on my face and snot stuffing up my nose.

Liam and Wes were right, I'm just a baby. A big kid wouldn't be crying in the dark corner of a closet hoping it'll all go away if you just wish hard enough. I bet Wes never cries. I know Lee doesn't.

"Come out now, Claire. Playtime is over."

"No," I cry louder. "Please don't make me."

"Now!" He growls as the closet door rattles. I gasp.

"Leave me alone!"

"Get out of the fucking closet, Claire!" He roars.

"Please no," I cry harder, my body shaking with each sob.

"When," he kicks his hard boots against the closet door and it shudders.

"Please."

"Are you," he kicks it again.

The doors are the kind with the slats that fold sideways. We have them at home and mama says I always pinch my fingers in the accordion. Whatever that is.

"I just wanna go home," I whisper.

"Gonna," he kicks again.

"I just want my mommy," I sob. "Please. I just want my mommy."

"Fucking," the boards snaps and I scream.

"I just wanna go home, please," I beg.

"Learn!" he shouts as he kicks the broken boards out of the way. He leans down and grabs me by my upper arms.

"Please," I wheeze but my words are cut short when he slaps my face hard. So hard I taste blood in my mouth and it's so yucky I feel sick. I'm going to throw up from the yucky taste. I try as hard as I can not to. I know that if I do, he'll punish me again. I don't want that. Anything but that.

"You are home, baby," he coos right before he slaps me again. I cry out again, falling to the floor with his last hit. It's so strong he knocks me down with it.

"And I thought I told you to call me daddy," he says as he lands a hard kick to my back.

"You're not my daddy, you'll never be my daddy," I whisper. "My daddy is a nice man. He would never hurt me. You'll never be my daddy," I say again but the bad man can't hear me, he already walked away. I have nowhere to go, but one thing is for sure, I have to escape.

"Claire!" someone shouts.

I wake up with a scream lodged in my throat, my heart is pounding with the need to run and the burn in my shoulder is telling me that I won't get anywhere fast.

"Claire!" someone shouts, and I realize it's Emma.

Emma is standing before me in my bedroom. What happened? I was asleep, I think. I look at the clock and realize that it's ten in the morning. I look back up at her and the worry for me that she's projecting out.

"I'm fine," I tell her.

"Okay," she says after she audibly swallows like a cartoon character and I realize that Emma knows me and Wes and Lee now, but she didn't know us then. She didn't know us when I was a kid lost and scared in the woods. She didn't know the guys as scared teens feeling guilty for not watching a little girl as closely as they should have. And now I can't help but think that Emma now knows maybe a little too much.

"So . . ." I start awkwardly. "What brings you by?"

"I heard you cut class, so I came to have a little fun too," she says. She's still shaken by what she walked in on but she's trying her best to bury it. I can appreciate that so I'm going to go along with it.

"I'm not cutting class, I was shot." I roll my eyes.

"Semantics." Emma shrugs.

"Won't Lee be pissed?" I ask.

"Who gives a shit what Captain Goodnite wants?" she snaps. "I don't. And I don't work for him. I work for the county at the discretion of the Mayor."

"Well then," I say thinking we could both use a day off. "I guess we're cutting class. What should we do?"

"Well, I was thinking that it's high time we finish planning this wedding," she says looking a little unsure of herself. Neither Emma nor I gave a shit about wedding planning, it was always Anna who wanted it to be a special day. Emma even once went so far as to say she would never get married. Also words I had previously spoken.

"Are you feeling alright?" I can't help but ask. Emma raises a brow in response to the question and the irony is not lost on me. But still . . .

"I'm fine," she shoots back my previous answer. "The place is booked, and invitations have been sent but you don't even have a dress. Or flowers. Or a cake." She ticks off on her fingers.

"We're kind of in poor shape when you put it like that."

"Exactly," she agrees obviously picking up steam to her cause.

"So where do we start?" I ask.

"The shore." The Jersey Shore. I haven't been there in years. This could be fun after all.

"Let me just get dressed and I'll be right down," I say drawing her attention to the fact that I am obviously naked under the sheets. I pull them up to my neck and embarrassment burns hot across my cheeks.

"Nice," she smirks. I just roll my eyes. It's on the tip of my tongue to ask her when the last time she's seen Lee was. I know they still hook up and it's even more traumatic than before, so I refuse to take the bait and throw it in her face. "I'll just go make some coffee."

I wait until after she leaves the room to jump up and hurry through my morning routine. I'm eager to start out on what might be my first fun day in ages. And with a friend too. I'm eager to shake off this cloak of death and sadness. Look at me attempting to be normal and shit!

We'll just overlook the recovering from a gunshot wound business . . .

chapter 7

the shore

IRUN INTO MY closet and stand there for a moment unsure of what to wear. It's been a long time since I didn't have to get up and get ready for a day at work. The last time, I didn't have to head to the station for any length of time was the last time I was injured. I pretty much lived in leggings and t-shirts. In fact, that's exactly what I was wearing the night Wes proposed.

He was so handsome, standing there on the deck in the backyard, surrounded by twinkle lights and flowers. Soft music played, and he had a feast laid out for us on the patio table. Wes had on worn jeans and a button-down shirt with the sleeves rolled back. *Hello, arm porn!* His feet were bare as he stood there before me and told me he loved me, he had always loved me, and he always would.

We danced to Ed Sheeran soft and slow in the grass as he slowly sank down onto one knee and asked me to marry him. He wants to be my partner and lover, my light in the darkness and while I know that it is unfair to bring him into my own personal hell, I also couldn't imagine then and I can't imagine now a time when I wouldn't love Wes with all of my heart. So, I looked into his whiskey colored eyes and said yes.

Wes slipped the mother of all diamond rings on my finger—the one that I have worn every day since—and then he made love to me right there in the backyard under the late afternoon sky. It is by far one of my favorite memories. I let my right-hand drift over to my left to touch the center stone on my ring like a lodestone. It guides me back to center. I don't need the ring or the fanfare, I just need Wes.

Emma was wearing jean shorts and a ribbed tank top when she blasted into my bedroom this morning so that is exactly what I will wear. I pull on light jeans shorts over my bra and panties, but instead of a fitted tank, I opt for a loose fitting vee neck tank in white. I slide a pancake holster into the back of my shorts before checking the magazine on my side arm. I load a round into the chamber before locking it into my holster.

Yesterday might have been a one off, but on the chance that it wasn't, I'd rather be safe than sorry.

I slide my feet into a pair of converse sneakers and pick up my badge. I realize that I don't have anywhere to stick my shit, so I dig through the back of my closet for a small designer bag that Anna had gifted me years ago and stuff my badge, my wallet, and cellphone in it. I look at all rebe extra space in there and toss in a few hair ties and my drop gun for good measure before slinging its long strap across my body.

I take the stairs slower than usual because the concussion, while mild as it may be, has me singing the national anthem in my head to keep from puking while the room spins. I want to go back to work as soon as possible and falling down the stairs in my own home won't exactly tell Wes and Lee that I'm ready for battle.

Emma is furiously texting someone on her phone but pauses to look up at me when she sees me. I feel her appraising look and know that she is taking stock of everything wrong with me, probably to report back to Wes.

"A purse?" she asks me on a raised eyebrow.

"What?" I ask mildly offended. "I can't carry one?"

"No," she answers. "You can't. How many guns do you have in there anyway?"

I'm a little wounded that she sees through me so thoroughly. I kind of don't want to answer her. She'll be unbearable, really.

"Just one," I say with my head held high.

"And in total?" she asks me as she scans my carefully chosen outfit. "How many do you have on you over all?"

I let out a heavy sigh. "Just the usual two," I answer.

"Oh good." She smiles a wicked smile. "Me too. Let's roll!"

I laugh and shake my head at her. "You're ridiculous," I tell her.

"But I'm your ridiculous."

"This is true." I sigh. When Emma is like this, when her sense of humor and her uniqueness shine through, I know exactly why my brother fell in love with her. I just hope one day they figure it all out because life is so short.

"Whatever." She rolls her eyes. "You love me. Now let's go get you married!"

"Alright."

We walk through the front door and I push the button to lock it behind us before climbing into her white Jeep Cherokee. Emma turns the key in the ignition and fires her up. Taylor Swift singing about someone making you do something that you shouldn't blasts through the speakers. I look at Emma through the corner of my eye. She is full of surprises these days.

She reaches over to the dashboard to turn the volume down.

"What?" She shrugs a shoulder. "I love me some T-Swift."

"I don't doubt that," I tell her as she cranks up the volume and pulls out of my neighborhood on two wheels as I change the subject. "So, have you got any info on the downtown shooting?"

"Uhn-uhh," she denises me. "No way. Today is wedding shit and fun only—and maybe, just maybe, if you're really really good, a funnel cake—but no murder or mayhem talk."

"Come on," I plead with her. "Wes won't tell me anything."

"That's alright," she says when the song ends effectively changing the subject. "I have prepared a prenuptial planning musical snack for you."

"Should I even ask?" I shoot her the side eye.

"Of course," she laughs before switching playlists.

I can't help but laugh as I hear the opening chords to Blondie. Emma and I sing the entire *Bridesmaids* soundtrack all the way down to the shore. There is a lightness in my chest that hasn't been there in a long-time and I have Emma to thank for that. She's truly a wonderful friend.

By the time Emma pulls into one of the paid parking lots by Seaside Heights my chest hurts from laughing so hard and my eyes are wet from crying, not from sadness but laughter. Finally. After all this time, my heart still hurts so very much.

"Here's our first stop," she says as she turns the ignition off.

"Where are we?" I ask as I look around.

"I figured, we'd get the shit part over first," Emma says as she looks around. She audibly swallows down what looks like . . . fear before finishing on a whisper. "You know? Rip it off like a band aid."

When I look at the big marquee sign over the shop that we are parked directly across from I can't help but throw my head back and laugh. Emma looks to me quickly and a scowl pulls at her brow.

"Come on." I laugh. "It can't be that bad."

"You don't know that!" she shouts.

"Do you have any colors in mind?" I ask as we push open our doors and step down from her Jeep.

"Anna wanted pink," she says softly as we head into the bridal shop. So, that's how it's going to be? Alright, I can handle that. Pink it is.

Bells tinkle as we push open the door and a young woman, probably in her early twenties, dressed in slacks and a sweater twinset. She has a tiny bit of a maniacal gleam in her eyes but I would probably look like a sociopath if I had to work in wedding hell all day, every day too.

"Hello and welcome to Fairytale Brides!" she greets us enthusiastically. "My name is Destiny and I like to think that makes me pretty darn qualified to help you plan your magical day. Now, who is the lucky bride?"

"She is," Emma says catching me off guard as she shoves me into the slightly desperate clutches of Bridal Barbie.

"But she is my maid of honor," I rally, trying to turn the attention away from me. "Her name is Emma and she loves the color pink!" How is this girl allowed in the state of New Jersey? She is too perky for any self-respecting Jersey girl.

"Yes!" Destiny fist pumps the air. "I just knew I was going to love you girls. Pink. Is. Awesome!"

Emma drags her index finger across her neck in a throat cutting motion as Destiny grabs her by the hand and drags her down an aisle of racks completely covered in pink dresses and mouths to me, "You're dead. Sleep with one eye open, Goodnite."

"Bring it."

"So, were we thinking long or short?"

"Fancy," Emma answers. "We're doing this up right."

"Awesome!" Destiny squeals. "Where is the ceremony?"

"On the beach here at the shore," Emma answers as we watch with twin horrified expressions as she loads up her arms with what has to be a bare minimum of twenty pink dresses.

"Right this way, Moe," Destiny calls over her shoulder.

"No," Emma says looking a little pissed. "My name is Emma. Not Moe."

Destiny just laughs before explaining, "No silly. Not Moe, MOH—Maid of Honor."

"Ohhh," Emma and I both say at the same time. We are so out of our league here.

"Let's just get you in a fitting room," Destiny says as she pulls open a mirrored door.

"I'll . . . uhh . . . I'll just wait for you out here," I stammer as the mirrored door slams in my face, blocking out the disgruntled frown of my very best friend.

"Benedict Arnold," I hear her gripe from the other side of the door.

I sit on a beautiful, yet grotesquely uncomfortable upholstered chair just outside of the fitting rooms. I hear a rustling and then a groan come from within the dressing room.

"Everything . . . okay," I call out hesitantly.

"Oh, just peachy," Emma responds.

"No, this is really more of a cotton candy than a peach," I hear Destiny correct Emma and I can't help the snicker that escapes my mouth.

"I heard that!" Emma snaps.

"Oh, come on out," I say. "It can't be that bad."

"Oh, it can," Emma says.

"Come out and let me see."

"Un uh."

"Please . . ." I beg.

"No."

"It's my wedding," I challenge.

"I hate you," she says before she opens the door. I am willing to admit that I am wholly unprepared for the sight that greets me—my dear friend in a bright pink strapless monstrosity. I want to laugh but I know Emma is armed so I rein it in.

"That's . . ." I start. "Not that one."

"Thank God," Emma mumbles before heading back into the fitting room.

I lean back in my seat thinking that this day might not be so much fun after all. That dress was truly terrible and by the horrified expression on Emma's beautiful face and the stack of pink that I had seen Destiny drape over her arms, I'm not thinking such good things about the rest of this dress search.

The mirrored door opens again, and I look up. Emma is wearing a hot pink strapless dress with a knee length hemline and enough tulle underneath to make rockabilly dreams come true. It has a wide black belt around her narrow waist. The dress is awful but apparently, my bff has a banging body. No wonder she brings all the boys to the yard.

"No," I say before she even steps out of the dressing room.

"God bless you," she sighs as she turns on her heel.

The next hour is spent in more of the same. One terrible dress after another when my phone chimes with a text in my purse.

WES: How goes the day of rest?

Huh? How is my day off going? I can't say that I'm resting because I'm not. I should be truthful, but the truth often gets me into hot waters where Wes is concerned. I am just about to fabricate the truth with a little white lie when I realize that big bastard has probably already tracked my phone. Damn find my friends app.

```
ME:   Not   resting?   I'm   dress
shopping with Emma.
```

The little typing bubbles pop up right away, so I know that he was waiting for my response.

```
WES: I know, I already tracked
your phone and called Emma.
```

That sneaky bastard! I just knew it! My fingers fly over the keys on the screen of my phone.

```
ME: I knew it! That's a little
shady even for you, Fed.
```

The little bubbles pop up immediately again.

```
WES: It is and I'm sorry. I'll
make it up to you tonight.
```

Color me curious. My interest is peaked.

```
ME: How?
```

```
WES: You can sit on my face to-
night.
```

Yep, that'll do it. That's the ball game, folks.

```
ME: Apology accepted.
```

```
WES: Seriously, what are you
doing?
```

ME: Planning our wedding and carrying a purse!!!

The text bubble pops up again and then disappears only to pop up again. They vanish again before showing one more time. Wes must be confused by my response because it would seem that he is typing, deleting, typing, deleting over and over again.

WES: Wonders never cease with you.

I roll my eyes at the screen. It makes the light throbbing in my temple gain some momentum.

ME: Ha Ha. *Slow clap*

WES: Plan us a good wedding day, baby.

I can see the smile on his face in my head. Wes loves the idea of us finally getting our happily ever after. And if I'm being totally honest, so do I.

ME: Okay.

WES: See you tonight.

I am just putting my phone back into my bag when I hear the door click open one more time and there stands Emma looking like a fairy princess . . . no a queen. Emma looks like a Grecian goddess with her strawberry curls piled up loosely on top of her head. The dress she's wearing is gathered high on her clavicle with a narrow cut exposing her muscular shoulders. The dress skims her lush curves and falls at her feet. When she does a little pirouette before me I can see that the entire back is open. It's pink but such a soft whisper of the hue that it's almost silvery setting off her pale skin.

"Well . . ." she says unsure of herself. "What do you think?"

"You're gorgeous," I whisper while staring at her. Emma tucks a lock of hair behind her ear in an unusual show of vulnerability.

"Don't joke," she says quietly.

"I'm not kidding. This is the dress."

"Are you sure?" she asks me hesitantly.

"Yeah," I answer her. "Do you like it?"

"I feel . . . pretty."

"Then this is the one," I tell her.

"I had a feeling . . ." Destiny says peeking around Emma. "Let me just get these castoffs out of the way and you can change back when you're ready, MOH."

"Yeah, Moe," I tease. "I just want to look at you for a bit."

"Me too."

Emma and I stand there—her on the carpeted platform and me behind her—just staring at her in the mirror lost in all the beauty that is Emma. And she is beautiful. Medium height and curvy with strawberry blonde hair and green eyes that hold a little bit of sadness just beyond their surface, but then again, don't we all.

I startle when an avalanche rolls towards us in the bridal shop. I don't realize that it's Destiny until the avalanche starts talking.

"It's your turn next, bride!" she cheers enthusiastically.

I can help the groan that slips out from between my lips. Emma throws her head back and laughs.

"I'll just change really quick," she says as she hops down from the platform and hurries into her dressing room clutching her long skirt in her hands. "I wouldn't want to miss this."

"I heard that!" I shout as a now empty-handed Destiny herds me into another room that's hidden beyond the mirrored door.

As soon as the latch clicks closed she is pulling my clothes off and I'm a little alarmed at how fast she does it.

"Oh dear," she says when she uncovers my holster.

"I'm a police officer," I say quietly not wanting to startle anyone else in the bridal salon.

"It's okay," she says. "I'll just let you handle that real quick." And I do, stuffing it down into my purse.

I turn back and she's holding open a dress for me to step into and when I do, Destiny is pulling it up to cover my body and fastening it closed at my back.

"Oh boy," I mumble not sure what I'm looking at.

"Come out, bitch!" Emma calls from the other side of the door.

"Uhh . . ." I stammer.

"Oh no," she barks from outside. "I did it now you have to. That's the deal."

"I was shot!" I bargain.

"I don't care. Get your happy ass out here."

"I can't wait until you get married," I snap.

"Well don't hold your breath sister, because it will be a cold day in hell before that happens."

"You don't know that," I sigh as I push open the door and step out. Emma has her mouth hanging open. This dress really must be that bad.

She pulls her phone out of her purse and snaps a quick picture.

"Hey!" I shout.

"Now go take that off, it's awful," she orders. I catch Destiny biting her lip to keep from laughing at Emma and me. Maybe she's not so bad after all.

We head back into the dressing room and after a huge stack of dresses that was one bad after another, I am just about to quit.

"This is hopeless," I whine to Destiny. My shoulder is starting to burn and I'm tired and cranky. Emma looks gorgeous in her dress and I look stupid in every single dress. I want to cry, and I *never* cry! And I'm starving. I need tacos and I need them now.

"I have one more I want you to try," she says to me.

"I don't know . . ." I hedge.

"These were terrible, I admit," she says taking a deep breath. "But this one will be the right one. I can feel it. Trust me one more time?"

"Just one more," I tell her. "Then I'm getting tacos. This has been a taco kind of day."

Destiny laughs before grabbing the last dress off of the hanger and holding it open for me to step into it. She pulls it up as soon as I step into it. I slide my arms in and she quickly does up the hidden zipper. I turn and look at myself in the mirror and freeze. I'm not looking at me, but someone beautiful. She's soft and feminine—*delicate*—and everything I want to be. At least on my wedding day.

"Well," Emma calls. "Don't keep me waiting."

"Trust me," Destiny says on a smile as she pushes open the dressing room door for me to step through. "It was well worth the wait."

"Fuck me," Emma mumbles as I climb up onto the platform and look over my shoulder at her. "She's right. You're beautiful."

"I feel beautiful."

I turn and look back at myself in the mirror. The dress has a deep vee in the front and sleeveless. The nude illusion fabric covers the bandage on my shoulder. White, gauzy fabric is delicately wrapped over my breasts making me look like I have a generous amount of cleavage but in a tasteful way. The skirt is miles and miles of soft, filmy layers of sheer, white fabric that flows out around me in the prettiest way. The back is a vee cut down to just about my ass and a spray of tiny, white flowers from over my left shoulder and down across my waist and again down the back to add just the right amount of decoration.

"This is it," Emma says softly. "This is the one."

"It is," I agree before turning back to Destiny. "I'm afraid to ask how much it is though."

"It's actually paid for," she tells me making my own jaw drop down.

"What?" I ask. "That can't be right."

"It is," she assures me. "I checked your file when Emma called to schedule this appointment this morning. It's all be prepaid by a Dr. Anna Garner."

I feel my throat tighten and a burn behind my eyes. Anna.

"She paid for your dress, veil, MOH's dress and two more bridesmaids dresses and a flower girl," she tells us. "It's been paid for for months."

I'm sure it has been. The last thing Anna did before

she left this world was buy me my fucking wedding dress. A friend to the end and always a champion of my relationship with Wes. I look to Emma in the mirror and see her swallow the lump in her throat. He eyes are red rimmed and glassy just like I'm sure mine are.

"How did you find this place again?" I ask her.

"Anna chose it."

"Anna," I whisper.

"Yeah."

"Okay," I say shoring up my strength. "We'll take it all," I tell Destiny.

"Wonderful!" she cheers.

I look to Emma. "I need tacos . . . and tequila."

"Here, here," she responds softly. "Although we still have to pick out a cake."

"Chocolate," I tell her. "Wes loves chocolate cake."

"Chocolate cake it is then," Emma agrees. "Now let's see about those tacos."

Emma and I chose flowers over tacos and margaritas that I probably shouldn't have mixed with the Tramadol the ER doc prescribed—or as I like to call it, fuck it all, because it knocks me on my ass and then some—but who's looking?

After lunch, she took me to buy the most ridiculous pair of heels known to man and I hate them instantly.

"You can't wear those big clunky boots on your big day," Emma reminds me.

"I'm not," I inform her kicking out a sneaker clad foot. "Today, I'm wearing sneakers."

"You can't wear those ratty assed shoes either."

"They're not ratty!" I defend my favorite off duty shoe.

"Half of the heel is missing on your left foot!"

"Oh . . . whoops."

"Yeah, whoops," she mimics me with her arms folded across her chest. "Now walk!"

I scrape my feet across the floor in the shoe department of this high-end department store. I stumble a little. The stilettos on these heels are impossibly high.

"I'll never be able to walk in these," I cry.

"That's why you have to practice," Emma says to me the way that one would scold a whiny child.

I let out a sigh and begin walking again. Lost in my own thoughts of impending doom when Emma breaks the silence on my trek across the floor once more.

"You have to admit the shoes are really sexy."

"They are," I agree on a sigh. They are ornately beaded swirls of silver beads over nude pointed toe pumps with mile high stilettos.

"I imagine Wes will have a field day with them," she tosses out filling my head of images of Wes's face when he strips off my gorgeous gown to find my wedding lingerie and these heels underneath.

Or maybe he won't even peel my dress down . . . maybe Wes will just fuck me dress and all. The imagery sends a shiver up my spine and I pick up my pace suddenly able to master these shoes like Tyra on a catwalk.

"That's what I thought," she says. "We'll take them."

chapter 8

safe and warm

I'M SITTING ON THE old recliner that Wes loves in the darkening living room as the sun goes down beyond the windows. I have an afghan my gran knitted across my legs and an iPad in my hands. I'm reading a trashy historical romance that my mom swore would heal me from the inside out.

"This highlander wields his penis like he wields his claymore," she had said this afternoon when she called me to tell me that she had sent her favorite book to my account. Although she whispered the word *penis*. "If that doesn't heal you, I don't know what will."

"Mom," I had laughed into the phone. "I'll check it out. Thanks for thinking of me."

"Of course," she had said before continuing. "Wes will thank me. I find them . . . inspiring."

"Mom." I laugh. "I'm not sure I need to know these things."

"What?" she had asked with the air of innocence in her voice that she lacked in real life. "It's true and you're almost a married woman. You're going to have to learn to keep things spicy."

"Trust me, Wes doesn't have any trouble keeping things spicy," I had mumbled.

"Well," she had laughed. "Good to know. I'm glad you're feeling better, baby girl. I'll talk to you real soon."

"Alright, mom. I love you."

"And I love you," she had said before she hung up.

That was over and hour ago. I downloaded the book right away and have been lost in it ever since. She was right, our highlander does wield both his penis and his claymore with excellent precision. I had no idea that historical romances could be so . . . steamy.

The lock on the door clicks and I immediately look around like I am guilty. I guess I'm embarrassed to be caught reading a sexy romance novel.

"What's going on here?" Wes asks immediately taking the temperature of the room. My eyes are so wide that it feels like one of my eyeballs might pop out.

"Nothing."

"What were you doing?" he asks me.

"Oh, just reading."

"Sure," he says shutting the front door behind him and twisting the lock. "What were you reading?"

"Just a book."

"I gathered that," Wes says with a raised eyebrow. "Mind if I take a look?"

I let out an eep. "No, don't do that."

He watches me for a moment rolling up his cuffs as he moves deeper into the room. "Have you eaten?"

"No. I waited for you," I say nervously. "I'm sorry. I didn't start anything. I wasn't sure when you would be home." Why am I so nervous?

"Don't apologize," he says before planting a soft kiss on my forehead. "You were supposed to be resting today. Want to come talk to me while I fix something quick?"

"Sure."

I follow Wes into the kitchen and watch as he pulls chicken breasts out of the fridge along with vegetables. He pulls oil and a skillet from the cabinet.

"Can I do anything to help?" I ask.

"Sure thing," he says before picking me up and setting me on the island to sit next to the cutting board where he laid out the vegetables.

Wes heats up the oil in the skillet before placing the chicken breasts into the pan. He moves over to the island and picks up a knife cutting salad vegetables while he stands next to me. His elbow brushes my thigh every so often sending tingle up my spine and heat to other places.

Mom was right about the book. I'm feeling inspired.

"So, what were you reading?" he asks me softly.

"Oh, this and that," I answer as vaguely as possible while feeling the blush heat my cheeks and travel down my neck.

Wes dumps the vegetables into a big, blue glass bowl. He sets the salad over on the other counter before dumping the cutting board and knife into the sink.

"So pretty," he rumbles as he traces a fingertip down my neck and over my chest just skirting my cleavage. "I love it when you blush."

"I'm not blushing," I lie.

"What were you reading?" he asks me again, crowding me in.

"It was nothing . . . really."

"Tell me," he whispers. "Please."

"It was a romance that my mom sent me," I admit.

"That doesn't sound too bad," Wes says as he steps between my legs. "What was it about?"

"A highlander." Wes smiles wicked.

"And what did this highlander do?"

"He wields a sword."

"Anything else?" Wes rumbles as he places open mouth kisses against the side of my neck. His beard scraping my skin in delicious ways.

"He also wields a pretty powerful penis," I admit when Wes scrambles my brain with his mouth.

"Is that so?"

"Yeah," I breathe as he moves his hand up underneath my blousy tank top to burn against the bare skin of my belly.

"I bet we can do better than that," he says with confidence.

"Oh yeah?"

"Yeah, baby," he says as he unsnaps the button on my shorts. "Lay back."

I do as Wes asks laying back on the cool stone of the kitchen island. He pushes my tank up exposing the skin of my belly and places soft kisses there as he unzips my shorts and pulls them from my body.

"So wet," he tells me as he touches his fingertips to the gusset of my panties before pulling them down my legs. "Is this for the highlander or for me?"

"You," I tell him as he traces my opening with the tip of his index finger.

"That's fucking right." He sinks that finger deep into my pussy and I want it and so much more.

"Wes." My breath catches in my throat as he pulls his finger from between my legs and sucks it deep into his mouth, keeping his deep whiskey eyes locked on mine. Wes says nothing as he pops that finger free and then unbuttons the buttons down the front of his Fed dress shirt before letting it fall to the floor. "Please."

But that's the last coherent thing I say as he leans over, putting his mouth on me. He licks me like a starving man. All the air is sucked out of my lungs as he flicks my clit with his tongue over and over never letting up, never letting me catch my breath. Wes's scruff abrades my inner thighs

I arch my back against the stone countertop, the cool marble a harsh contrast to the way that Wes is heating my body from the center out.

Wes drags his lips down my thigh as he thrusts two fingers deep into my center but it's just not enough.

"I-I need," I pant.

"I know what you need, baby," Wes says as he pushes to his feet to stand over me.

Wes unbuckles his belt and unhooks his pants. The sound of his zipper going down is drowned out by the pops of the chicken as it sizzles in the pan but when he pushes his pants and boxers briefs down, letting his hard cock spring free to bob between us thick and heavy, I could care less about the chicken.

"Wes." I roll my bottom lip into my mouth and nip

at it as I watch Wes pump his hard length in his fist.

"Do you want my cock or a highlander's?" he asks me as he notches the tip to my opening.

"Yours," I pant desperately. "Only yours."

My correct answer is rewarded when Wes drives home in one long, hard thrust. I let out a groan release my lip from my teeth.

Wes leans forwards on his elbows on either side of me. He grinds his hips into me as he drives forward. Each slow thrust is accentuated by a swivel of his hips.

"Your highlander might turn you on, baby," he says as he slides in again.

"Yes," I pant.

"But it's my cock that makes you come."

"Yes."

Wes slides his hand up the side of my body and pinches my nipple between his fingers as he palms my breast before leaning down to take it in his mouth. I arch my back and let him take it as he slides deep, hitting a secret spot deep inside.

Wes lets his teeth scrape against my nipple as he lets it slide free from his mouth. He slides his arms underneath my back spearing me deeper onto his cock, pulling us upwards so that I'm sitting on the edge of the counter as he powers into me again and again.

I wrap my arms around his shoulders and hang on tight as he drives faster and faster.

"I love you so much," he says against my mouth.

"I-I love you," I pant.

As he drives his cock faster and faster, harder and harder into me I know that I'm close, so so close. It won't take much to push me over the edge.

"I-I'm going to—" I start

"Come now. Give it to me."

Wes presses his mouth to mine absorbing the noises that are coming from my mouth as I fly over the edge. Wes is right behind me thrusting one more time before planting himself deep as he lets go and comes inside me.

Wes places soft kisses to one corner of my mouth and then the other, over each of my eyelids, and then finally over my mouth. I open underneath him and let him lick in. Wes breaks our kiss to drop his forehead to mine.

"Thank the highlander for me." He laughs.

"I think . . ."

"Yeah, baby?"

"I think I'm going to buy you a kilt for a wedding present." At that, Wes throws his head back and laughs. The chicken mostly burned to the pan behind us.

Wes kisses me—quickly but passionately—one more time before sliding free from my body and doing up his pants letting his belt hang open.

"I'm just going to lay here and die," I inform him while I'm spread out like a starfish on the large island in the kitchen.

To that, the love of my life just smirks, smug bastard that he is and all.

"Well this doesn't look so good," Wes says from somewhere behind me. I tip my head back and to the side to see that he is poking at the chicken breasts in the pan with a spatula.

"I'm sorry to say it," I tell him. "But those look like a done deal."

"I'm sorry." Wes sighs.

"No, don't apologize. It was worth the sacrifice. I mean . . . I enjoyed myself."

"I know." Wes smirks at me again. I roll my eyes.

"You are truly ridiculous."

"I know that too," he tells me. "But I'm your ridiculous."

"That is true."

"Still planning on laying there naked?" Wes asks me.

"Yeah, pretty much," I answer. "Why?"

"Because this chicken is raw on one side and charcoal on the other. The whole thing is going in the trash."

"Ok," I start to respond feeling confused. "What does that have to do with my lack of clothing?"

"Because I'm calling in a pizza and I didn't know if you wanted the kid who delivers to see you in the altogether. I mean, on the one hand, I won't have to tip him because you'll be the tip, but on the other hand, I'll have to kill him because he's going to want to give you more than just the tip and he's not giving you anything."

"That was the most convoluted diatribe I have ever heard."

"Are you going to put on pants or does little Jimmy have to die tonight," Wes says on a raised eyebrow.

"His name isn't even Jimmy!" I shout throwing my hands out to my sides as I sit up on the counter.

"Well, then what is it?" Wes challenges me.

"How the hell should I know?"

"Pants or death?"

I shoot Wes a death glare. "I guess I should go find

some pants . . ."

"That's what I thought," he chuckles as he swats me on the ass when I bend over to snatch his dress shirt up off of the floor.

"I'm freaking going!" I shout as I hop off of the counter and head for the door.

"Hey Claire," he calls after me. I stop walking out of the room and turn to look at him.

"What is it, Wes?"

"But I'm not wrong, baby."

I just turn back around and start walking again and mumble, "I better get extra pepperoni and sausage out of this."

"I'll get you your extra pepperoni, baby," his sex rough voice rumbles over my skin even from across the room. "But I've got all the sausage you could need right here."

And he's right. He does.

I quickly make my way down the hall to the bathroom. I slip my arms into Wes's shirt and button a few buttons but that's it. He's so tall that it falls to my knees. I'm covered in case the pizza delivery kid catches a glance. I pull a hair band that I have stashed in the drawer out and toss my hair up in a messy bun on top of my head. I look in the mirror and see dark tendrils of my hair hang soft and loose around my flushed cheeks. Apparently good sex agrees with me.

I walk back out of the bathroom and Wes freezes in his tracks when he sees me. Good. He deserves to be teased a little.

"That's not quite what I had in mind," he tells me on a raised brow.

I shrug. "It's good enough."

"Good enough to get poor Jimmy maimed or killed?"

"That's up to you, dear. You know I'd never stand in the way of your evil plans . . ." I let the twinkle in my eyes show him that I'm teasing.

"Dangerous game, darling," he says following my lead.

I shrug again letting the game slip away. "I just like your shirts."

Wes's face goes soft before he answers me. "Far be it from me that I should ever deny you anything."

I just nod once.

"But I will take it back whenever I want," Wes warns me.

"Or you could just leave it on," I whisper. "There's nothing stopping you underneath."

Wes takes an instinctual step towards me when the doorbell rings. He clenches his fists at his side only to open them and then clench them again.

"We don't need pizza do we?" he asks me on a strangled voice.

"I'm starving," I say while shooting him my most innocent smile. "I can't survive on rabbit food alone."

"Of course, you can't," he mumbles under his breath before turning on his heel and answering the door.

I walk back into the kitchen and pull open the fridge. There is a bottle of wine in the back and tonight feels like a good wine night. I pour two glasses and place them on the counter shooting interested glances at the island countertop.

I dress the salad and am serving it onto plates when Wes walks back in carrying a giant pizza.

"My hero!" I cry draping the back of my hand across my forehead as if I might swoon.

"Hilarious," Wes drolls.

"I try." I bat my eyes making Wes smile and his whole face softens making him look younger.

"No pizza for you," he says as he lifts the box up over my head and out of my reach.

"What?!" I shout. "I didn't mean it. Give me my pizza back."

"Now tell me you love me . . ."

"I love you!"

"Now tell me I'm better than any highlander."

"You're so much better!"

"Here's your pizza," he says as he places the box on the island, pausing to look at where we were thirty minutes earlier. He slow blinks before turning back to me. "You know? I don't think I ever really appreciated this kitchen before . . ."

"Me either," I say before stuffing a giant bite into my mouth.

"What's on your mind, baby?" Wes asks me as I towel off my body. My skin is still bright pink from the hot water of my shower.

"It was just a long day."

"I thought it was a good day?" he asks me as he

wraps his arms around me pulling me in close as he rests his chin on top of my head. I love when he does this. I'm fairly tall for a woman so the fact that he is tall enough to make me feel small and delicate is kind of nice.

"It was," I begin to explain. "We found out Anna prepaid for all of the dresses right before she died. That was tough on us both."

"Did you pick out a dress?"

"Yeah," I say softly knowing that there is a wistful quality to my voice.

"Is it pretty?" he asks me. His voice is quiet in the still evening of our bathroom.

"Yeah," I sigh. "And kind of sexy too."

"Sexy?" Wes asks me. "Tell me about it."

"Unh uh," I decline.

"No?" I can hear the smile in his voice.

"No. I want you to be surprised."

"Okay, honey," he says toying with a lock of my wet hair. "I'll be surprised."

"Okay."

"Anything else bothering you?" he asks me.

"I can't stop thinking about Rodriguez," I admit.

"Yeah," he agrees. "Me too."

"Any new information?" I ask grasping at anything Wes might be willing to give me. I have to know what happened. I have this driving need inside of me to find the answer and solve the puzzle.

Wes studies me for a moment before letting out a heavy sigh. I know in that instant that he is about to give me the truth, whatever that might be.

"We have nothing," he says and the vein at his

temple pulses. I can tell how angry that makes him. It makes me angry too. "There are no tapes, no notes, no faces. We have nothing."

"I hate this," I whisper.

"Me too, honey."

Wes pulls the towel from around my body and places it on the bathroom counter before rolling up one of his t-shirts and dropping it over my head. I push my arms through the armholes as he lets the faded fabric drop around my thighs.

"Let's go to bed," he tells me holding out his hand for me to take it and I do without hesitation.

Wes walks me towards our bed and drops my hand only to pull the bedding back so that we can climb in. Wes pulls me into the safety of his arms after pulling the blankets back over us. I feel warm, and safe, and sleepy so I let myself drift off.

It wouldn't be until days later that I would realize that I was never safe.

chapter 9

go gray

"COME OUT OF THE closet, baby."

"No," I whisper, tears hot on my face and snot stuffing up my nose.

Liam and Wes were right, I'm just a baby. A big kid wouldn't be crying in the dark corner of a closet hoping it'll all go away if you just wish hard enough. I bet Wes never cries. I know Lee doesn't.

"Come out now, Claire. Playtime is over."

"No," I cry louder. "Please don't make me."

"Now!" He growls as the closet door rattles. I gasp.

"Leave me alone!"

"Get out of the fucking closet, Claire!" He roars.

"Please no," I cry harder, my body shaking with each sob.

"When," he kicks his hard boots against the closet door and it shudders.

"Please."

"Are you," he kicks it again.

The doors are the kind with the slats that fold sideways. We have them at home and mama says I always pinch my fingers in the accordion. Whatever that is.

"I just wanna go home," I whisper.

"Gonna," he kicks again.

"I just want my mommy," I sob. "Please. I just want my mommy."

"Fucking," the boards snaps and I scream.

"I just wanna go home, please," I beg.

"Learn!" he shouts as he kicks the broken boards out of the way. He leans down and grabs me by my upper arms.

"Please," I wheeze but my words are cut short when he slaps my face hard. So hard I taste blood in my mouth and it's so yucky I feel sick. I'm going to throw up from the yucky taste. I try as hard as I can not to. I know that if I do, he'll punish me again. I don't want that. Anything but that.

"You are home, baby," he coos right before he slaps me again. I cry out again, falling to the floor with his last hit. It's so strong he knocks me down with it. "And I thought I told you to call me daddy," he says as he lands a hard kick to my back.

"You're not my daddy, you'll never be my daddy," I whisper. "My daddy is a nice man. He would never hurt me. You'll never be my daddy," I say again.

"I am your daddy!" he roars as the wooden slats splinter inward.

I'm stuck, trapped under the broken pieces of wood and chips of paint from the closet door. I scream when the pieces of wood go flying towards my face and reach up to cover my head with my arms. Maybe it will save me from the sound beating I'm about to get but I know that it won't.

I have nowhere to go, but one thing is for sure, I have to escape.

I scream again.

"Claire!" he's shouting my name.

"No," I cry. "I won't come out. You can't make me."

"Claire."

"Please, I'll be good, I promise. I just want to go home," I plead as hot tears pour down my cheeks, my eyes are still firmly closed to the bad man.

I know when I open my eyes that I will see his mean face and I don't want to. No! I have to. I have to know who the bad man is.

"Claire."

I open my eyes and I look up at him expecting to see his mean face but all I see is a blur. No! I have to know who the bad man is.

"Claire, please come back to me," Wes's rough voice pleads. It cracks with emotion.

I blink my eyes trying to clear my mind whether it's a waking nightmare or the truth is left to be determined.

"Wes?" I ask hesitantly. I'm wrapped safely in the cocoon of his arms.

"Thank God," he rumbles before answering me.

"Yeah, baby. It's me."

"Okay," I whisper. "I think I had a nightmare."

"I know, honey," he says as he brushes the sweat dampened hair back from my forehead and around my face. "Can you tell me about it?"

This is what I love about Wes. He doesn't push me for more in these moments. He does not demand that I give him the information that I don't have or can't bear to give him. He just asks patiently and then sits back and waits for me to offer up anything or everything— or even nothing at all.

"I-I think . . ."

"Yeah?" he asks.

"I think I remember dark hair," I tell him hesitantly. "I think he had dark hair. The man who took me had dark hair."

"That's great, honey."

"But that's all I remember. When I look up into his face all that I see is a blur."

"But that's something. You're remembering and that's huge. The information will come, it just depends on when," Wes reassures me.

"But what if I never remember who he is or was?" I ask admitting one of my biggest fears.

"Then so what?" Wes shrugs his shoulders.

"What?" I ask unsure that I heard Wes correctly.

"So, what? Who cares if you never remember the details," Wes says. His voice growing in volume and determination to get his point across. "I don't care. I mean I do. I want you to have what you need to heal, but at the end of the day, I just want you."

"Wes—" I start but he interrupts me still on his

mission to make me see how much he really loves me.

"I want you in whatever package you might come in. So grow old, gain fifty pounds, let all that hair that drives me wild go gray. It'll still drive me wild when I'm eighty. My point is that none of that matters. I'm still going to love you like crazy and I'm still going to want to fuck you every night."

"Wes?"

"Yeah, baby?"

"I'm pretty sure that was sweet wrapped up in all of that vulgarity," I answer.

"It was," he answers me. "Remember, don't remember, it doesn't matter. What matters is at the end of the day it's you and it's me. The rest is just details."

And he's right. Wes is so very right. All of the bullshit is just that, bullshit, because at the end of the day, it's going to be just Wes and me and that is everything I will ever need to make it though.

"I love you, Wes." I reach up and place a soft kiss on his lips.

"I love you too," Wes tells me, his voice rumbling deep and rough in the still night. "How's the shoulder feeling?"

"Pretty good, why?" I ask.

"Because now I'm going to fuck you."

"Oh," I stammer.

"Yeah, 'oh.'"

And then Wes rolls me to my back covering my body with his. He covers my mouth with his and I happily open underneath his expert lips as he wedges his hips between my thighs and I readily accept him. Wes licks into my mouth as he rocks his hips to slide his cock back and forth through my wetness but never penetrating. His teasing drives me crazy and I arch my hips in an attempt to take him into my body.

"Not yet, greedy girl," he says after he tears his mouth away from mine. I let out a low whine at his opposition to what I currently want—what I need.

"Wes," I breathe.

He pushes the hem of his t-shirt up uncovering my thighs as he goes and then my hips. I hear his breath catch in his throat when he uncovers the juncture of my thighs where his slick cock pressed against my folds is there for us both to see.

"Wes, please," I plead.

"Not yet," he pants as he rocks his hips sliding the slick length of him against my clit. The motion sends sparks shooting off of my skin and I shudder at the contact causing Wes to stop moving again. "Soon."

Wes continues to push the hem of the t-shirt up and up and up exposing my belly button. He leans over and kisses and nips at the soft flesh that he uncovers. Wes glides his lips up and up following the trail that the t-shirt leaves in its wake until he reveals my breasts.

Wes scoops the t-shirt up and over my head in the same quick fashion that he had dropped it down around me for me to sleep in only a few hours earlier before tossing it over his shoulder to the floor. Then he places a soft kiss to my breast before teasing the nipple with a quick swipe of his tongue. I feel the sensation everywhere including where his cock is nestled to me.

Wes caresses my other breast with his heavy palm, running his thumb in maddening circles around my nipple as he sucks its twin into his mouth. He scrapes his teeth over the sensitive bud before soothing it with his tongue.

He lets my nipple slip from his mouth with a pop before kissing his way up my neck. All the while rocking his hips against mine. My breath seizes in my lungs when he scrapes his teeth against the side of my throat as he notches the tip of his cock to my opening.

"Wes," I pant as he slides in side.

"Yeah, baby," he answers my call in a rough rumble.

I arch my hips to make him go faster but—as always with Wes—he does things in his own time in his own way. I'm shaking, desperate for him to give me more. The slow and steady push and pull of his body and mine is slowly driving me mad.

"Wes—" I call out, but he doesn't hear me as he pumps inside me in his unhurried pace. "Wes, I-I need—"

"I know what you need," he says as he drives his cock in with a little more force.

"I need you," I answer as the head board rocks against the wall with an audible thump.

"Yeah," he rumbles again as he drives home this time a little faster but not by much. And yet, it's all I need. "You do, and I need you."

"You do?" I ask as I cling to his back my nails digging in as I hold on.

"With every breath I breathe, baby. I need you."

His words are all I need to send me over the edge. I tip my head back and call out as I do. This time Wes is right with me, coming with me. He drops his mouth to mine as he does, and I happily drink in his groan.

After a moment, Wes pulls out and rolls to the side taking me with him. He wraps me up in his arms.

"Think you can sleep now?" he asks me as he brushes my hair back from my face. I look up into his eyes and wonder what he must see when he sees me. I'm most likely a mess right now as I take stock of myself. I'm a little battered and bruised and now thoroughly fucked, but I'm okay.

"Yeah," I say softly. "I do."

"Good," he says as he tucks us back into bed not reaching for my discarded shirt.

I settle in and close my eyes. I let every muscle in my body relax one by one and every vertebra loosen in the same fashion. I am almost ready to drift off when Wes speaks to me one last time.

"Claire?" he asks, his voice soft in the midnight quiet.

"Yeah, Wes?"

"I won't pretend to know what's going on in your head with these nightmares . . . these memories . . . but baby?"

"Yeah?" I answer.

"You're safe with me."

"Okay, Wes."

"I mean it, Claire. You're safe with me and you're always going to be safe with me. Don't ever doubt it."

"I won't, Wes," I promise into the night.

"And baby?"

"Yeah?" I answer.

"I'm right where I want to be." His voice rings true with so much emotion packing its punch. With so much feeling that my heart pounds in my chest. "So, don't ever doubt that either."

"I won't."

"You're safe with me."

Those were the last words I heard before we both drifted off to sleep and I believed them with my whole heart. I believe in Wes and his strength and smarts and I believe in his heart that he loves me, and he would do anything to protect me. Even willing to lay down his own life for me.

But even Wes can't protect me from some monsters in the dark . . .

chapter 10

hamburger

BEEP . . . *BEEP* . . . *BEEP* . . .

Wes's alarm blares from the bedside table on his side of the bed. If it were mine, I would hit the snooze, but it's not. It sits like a sentry on his side of the table with the full knowledge that Wesley O'Connell who is everything that is good and right and dependable will not hit snooze and will shut it off.

I let out a weary sigh. Will I ever be as good as Wes? That's a question with an answer that will only come with time . . . and maybe some bourbon. Maybe I should go on one of those soul-searching adventures in a yurt in New Mexico . . . nah. Wes would never be on board to smoke some peyote and wait for the spirit animals of our ancestors to tell us the meaning of life.

I wonder what it's like to have sex in a yurt . . .

I rub the sand from my eyes as Wes reaches over to silence his alarm after not nearly enough sleep. I feel the bed shift underneath us as he rolls to face me.

"A penny for your thoughts," Wes asks me as he

brushes a lock of hair out of my eyes.

"I was wondering what it would be like to have you make love to me in a yurt."

Wes pauses for a moment appearing for all intents and purposes to be stunned. That's it, I finally broke him.

"What?" he laughs as he rolls me to my back with him on top of me settled between my thighs.

"I was thinking that this has been a tough year," I admit.

"Yeah, honey," he says, his face softening.

"So, I was wondering if maybe I should go on one of those spirit guide things in New Mexico," I continue.

"Okay?" Wes says waiting for me to finish my train of thought for the full story.

"But then I realized you probably aren't the kind of guy to smoke a bunch of peyote and then sweat in a yurt while we wait for the spirit animals of our ancestors to tell us what we're doing wrong."

"I don't think that's exactly how it goes on those trips," Wes says biting the inside of his cheek to keep from laughing.

"So, you do what to smoke peyote and sit in a yurt?" I ask him.

"Uhh . . . not exactly."

"That's what I thought. But then it got me to thinking about what it would be like to have sex in a yurt . . ."

Wes pulls the sheets up over our heads.

"I can probably answer some of your questions for you right now," he says to me. I see the heat in his eyes and like a moth to a flame I am drawn to him over and over again.

"Oh yeah?" I ask as I wiggle my hips underneath him. "I do have a few questions . . ." I trail off.

"Well let me see what I can do to set your mind at ease," Wes says as he rocks his hips sliding the length of his cock through my slit.

"Yes," I breathe.

"My beautiful Claire," he says as he rocks his hips again against me. "Always so wet for me."

"Yes."

"And only me," he says as the look on his face turns feral.

"Yes, only you." I moan as he thrusts inside.

I wrap my arms around his back and pull my knees up to my sides so that his strokes are deeper than before. We both moan at the new angle.

Wes places soft kisses all around my face and he gently glides in and out of my body as I rock my hips against his. It's soft and sweet and gentle and yet we need more.

"Wes?" I ask between shallow plunges of his cock

"Yeah, baby?" he asks as he slowly rocks back and forth between my legs.

"It was a flesh wound, honey," I tell him gently as he slows his pace to lie still with his hard cock still inside me. "I won't break."

"I know that," he says on closed eyes.

"Do you?" I ask him.

He sighs. "Yeah, I do." Slowly, he withdraws his length from me before slamming all the way in. "My girl needs to be fucked this morning."

He pulls almost all the way out before driving back in hard and fast.

"Yes," I pant.

Wes pulls all the way out before gripping my face in his hand, so I can't look away from him. His fingers digging into the flesh of my cheek and his thumb between my lower lip and chin. "You will tell me if anything hurts and we will stop immediately."

"Yes, Sir," I respond cheekily.

Wes lets go of my face before grabbing me by the hips and flipping me over onto my hands and knees. He shoves my upper body down into the mattress so only my ass is in the air.

The swat he lands to my backside rings out in the quiet room and I bite my lip as a rush of wetness floods my pussy.

"Don't give me any ideas that you aren't willing to follow through on, baby," he says, his voice raspy with sex and need. "I like it too much."

"Maybe I like it too," I admit as I look over my shoulder.

Wes dips two fingers into my pussy spreading my wetness around on his fingers before circling my asshole. "Yeah, I see that you do like it," he says as he sinks in a finger. "I wonder what else you might like?"

"Wes," I moan.

"I know, baby," he coos. "You need my cock."

"Yes."

He notches the tip of his cock to my pussy and slowly slides in. From this angle, with his finger in uncharted territory, I feel full. So full that it won't take much for me to come. Wes circles his hips as he slides back in and curls his finger.

"Oh, God."

"That's right, baby," Wes says as he pulls out and pumps back in, this time a little faster. "Soon I'm going to own this ass like I own this pussy and it's going to be so good."

But I can't think of the words coming out of his mouth while every brain cell I ever had is scrambling and rearranging. It's all that I can do to hang on to the edge of the mattress while Wes masters my body. This is exactly what I wanted and so much more.

"You're so close. I can feel it. The way your pussy grips my dick in all that wetness that's just for me. The way your body flushes and the way that you bite your lip. And those sexy as fuck noises that you make when you're about to give it all to me." He pumps his cock again and again, his other hand squeezing my ass cheek in his large palm the bite of it is almost enough to send me over.

"Yes."

"Let go, baby," he says as he thrust a little harder. "I'll catch you when you fall."

And I do.

"Wes!" I cry out as wave after wave crashes over me and I come harder than ever.

Wes pull his finger free and grips my ass cheeks in both hands. Hard.

"Yes!" he shouts. "That's it, baby." As he plunges in again and again harder and harder as my orgasm rolls over into another.

"Wes," I cry out.

"That's it," he growls as he pumps harder and faster. "Oh fuck, fuck, fuck, you feel so fucking good the way that you squeeze my dick." There is something about Wes's dirty talk that drives me absolutely wild.

"Yes."

"Yes! Again!" he demands.

"I-I don't know if I can," I cry out.

"You can!" Wes shouts as he powers his cock faster and faster, his fingertips biting so hard there's no doubt they'll leave bruises. "Give it to me."

"Yes," I moan, but I'm not sure if any words come out as he drives his cock deep and I scream as I come.

"Fuck fuck fuck, that's it, that's it, oh fuck, Claire!" he shouts as he plants his cock deep inside me and follows me over the edge.

Wes collapses on top of me and I love the feel of his weight pressing me into the mattress. The breath in our lungs sawing in and out of us in tandem.

After a moment he pushes up a little so that all of his weight isn't on me anymore but in truth, I never mind.

"Well," he rumbles after placing a tender open mouth kiss to the side of my neck making me smile. "Life with you will never be boring."

"I aim to please, Mr. O'Connell," I whisper.

"As do I, Mrs. O'Connell." He takes my earlobe into his mouth and nips just a little before letting is go and pulling out of me. "But now I really do need a shower and so do you."

"I do?" I ask.

"You do," Wes agrees. "I'm all for staking my claim on you, but even I wouldn't make you go into the station with sex hair and my cum drying on your thighs."

"I do appreciate the lack of caveman this morning," I tell him.

"Oh, I'm still a caveman for you, baby," he says as he skates his fingernail down my crack and over his new-found territory making my breath seize in my lungs. "But there is a time and place for it."

He reaches for me to help me up and I stand on shaky legs like a newborn giraffe. There's a smug twinkle in his eye that says he knows that he fucked me proper this morning. And, well, he did so I guess that smug look is earned.

"Let me shower you and then I'll drive you to work," he says. I sigh. Wes is really going to be unbearable to live with now.

"Okay," I say and then let him do just that.

It would seem that some lessons take longer to be absorbed. I guess I am going to have to make myself clearer—crystal fucking clear.

I hate that she drives me to this level of anger but that's on her not on me. She could have been mine all along, but no, she made a poor choice and now we all have to live with the consequences.

So instead of fucking my prize in my soft, warm bed this morning, I was out stealing a car. That's so . . . pedestrian. Such petty crimes are beneath a man like me, and yet here I am. I hate that she brings me down to this level.

I slowly drive past the side street where I know that police are stopped for lunch. A fucking hamburger. I shudder at the thought of such common food. I would never eat anything like that.

I circle back and drive again. I'm trying to get her attention. When I circle back again and pass her one more time, I know that I have. I wink as I watch her pick up her radio.

It's showtime!

I park this car on a side street. I won't be needing it anymore.

I head out on foot and walk directly up to the driver's side of the police car. There are two of them in the front seat eating lunch. Their styrofoam cartons in their laps and used napkins litter the dashboard. It's so filthy. Unsanitary.

She rolls down her window.

"Sir, can I help you?"

I smile wide and nod but don't answer her verbally. I casually paid a friend of a friend of a friend on the force with a coke problem to make sure that their body cameras didn't work this morning. But don't worry, he won't be in the way for long.

He looks up at me nervously, he knows what is about to happen because I explained everything to him this morning, but I don't acknowledge him.

"Sir, what can I do to help you?" she asks but it's already too late.

I pull the forty-five from the back of my pants and shoot her between the eyes. Before her partner can get a word out of his mouth I fire two rounds into his chest and one into his head. I neatly tuck the gun into the back of my pants and pull my jacket down low to cover it.

I smile at a small shopkeeper as I walk past and then head down the stairs to the subway. Just like any other anonymous man in America.

But soon, my queen, you'll know it's me because I'm coming for you . . .

Today sucks I'm so fucking bored.

I twirl in my rickety desk chair one more time. This morning when Wes dropped me off he made Liam, my fucking boss, promise not to let me do anything more strenuous than paperwork.

"You have got to be mother fucking kidding me!" I had shouted.

"Do you kiss her with that mouth?" Lee had asked Wes who had laughed, that big bastard.

"I do," he smiled, and I rolled my eyes. "But she's got other places I prefer to kiss."

"That's my sister and that's also disgusting," Lee groaned.

"Hey man, you started it," Wes said holding his arms out.

"Still gross," Lee said. "Now get out of my station."

"Gladly," Wes had said. "We have a deal?"

"Yep, it's like 1993 again and I'm babysitting my

little sister," Lee rolled his eyes.

"Yep, that's pretty much it."

"Don't I get a say at all here?" I asked.

"No!" They had both shouted.

"I hate you both," I had pouted as I crossed my arms across my chest.

"No, you don't," Wes said as he pulled me into his arms for a quick kiss. "You love me."

"Unfortunately," I sighed.

"Try and be good, babe," he laughed. The fucker. But I was too busy pouting. "I'll pick you up at five."

That was four freaking hours ago . . .

Now, I have completed every fucking page of busy work Lee had placed on my desk with a pat on my head and a thoroughly patronizing round of "be good," with a pat on my head.

I absolutely hate busy work. I get that the reports need to be filed, but no cop worth their weight wants to actually slow down and do the work to fill them out. We thrive off of being in the field and exist in a constant state of motion.

Filling out reports are neither of those.

I twirl in my chair one more time when the tones alert to another distress call. After the mass shooting the other day, the department captains got together and decided that all distress calls will automatically be patched in to all stations and all radios and cars.

What I hear next would chill me to my bones . . .

"*Did you see that?*" Officer Jasmine Alexander asks who I'm assuming is her partner, Matt Jerome. I have never gotten that warm and fuzzy feeling from him.

"*See what, Jazzy?*" he asks you can hear the frustration in his voice. "*You're imagining things.*"

Officer Alexander must have hit the distress code without alerting her partner which never means good things.

"*I'm not imagining things,*" she says. "*That car has driven by three times already. It's weird.*"

"*Just eat your burger, Jazzy.*"

"Hey, Matt—" she starts but he cuts her off.

"*Save it,*" he orders. "*Just eat your lunch so we can go back in service.*"

She clicks her microphone as if she is just relaying a call. "*Dispatch, a white, middle age male is approaching the vehicle.*"

"*Dispatch copies, respond with caution.*"

"*Sir, can I help you?*" she asks the unidentified male. After a pause where we can't hear him say anything Jasmine asks again. "*Sir, is there anything I can help you with?*"

There is nothing, but silence followed by a loud *pop* that can only mean one thing. The room is silent. And then another *pop, pop, pop* sounds.

"*Officer Alexander, do you copy?*" the dispatch officer shouts. "Officer Alexander, Officer Jerome, DO YOU COPY?"

Nothing. There is nothing. We all know that can only mean one thing.

"*All responding officers in the area, this is dispatch, please respond to shots fired on the corner of Main and Seventeenth. Car is no longer in service for dinner.*"

The room freezes before exploding, like a glass

windshield in a car crash. Officers and Detectives alike run at top speed out of the room. I jump out of my chair and catch Lee as he races out of his office palming his car keys. I grab him by the back of his arm and he whirls around on me.

"Take me with you," I demand.

"No."

"I'm not kidding, Lee!" I shout. I have to go with him, I have to be there because Jasmine was my friend.

"This isn't a game, Claire!" he shouts.

"You know I don't think this is a fucking game!" How dare he say such awful things. "You know that she was my friend!"

"You're injured," he argues with me.

"I've been cleared for duty and you're wasting time!" He is, and he knows it, I see the indecision warring on his face. Thank God my brother makes the right decision.

"Get in the car and don't fucking do anything stupid," he orders.

"I won't," I promise hoping that it isn't a lie.

I follow Lee out to his truck that looks identical to mine but it's new and the radio works. Unfortunately, he uses that to listen to a shit ton of Garth Brooks on the normal day, but today is anything but normal.

The car stays eerily silent as we drive across town. Silent as a tomb.

"We're going to have to walk in," he says to me. The scene has already been blocked off and all of the responding officers' vehicles are lining the available roadway.

"I'm up to it," I say as I catch a glimpse of the

black and white as we drive up a cross street and I feel the egg sandwich that I had for breakfast in the car on the way to the station this morning churning in my stomach. It's been a long time since I was sick at a crime scene.

But I guess today is a day of revisiting.

As we walk up the side street after Lee parks his department vehicle, I can't help but to remember the case that Jasmine and I worked on. My sister's murder, although at the time, I had no idea that Bonnie Bradley, a down and out forty-something single mother of three by day and down and out stripper by night was my half-sister, but now I do.

When we responded to the scene that night, she handled all of the dancers with extreme care and a pro-tectiveness that rivaled a mama bear. The young police officer impressed me right from the beginning. I was sure that her future was so bright and now it has been snuffed out—extinguished—forever.

It's incredibly unfair and if it's the last thing I do, I'm going to find out who did it.

chapter 11

bedlam

IT'S PANDEMONIUM.

When Lee and I turn the corner and approach the scene it's complete bedlam. People are screaming. While this neighborhood is not an affluent one, it is a relatively safe one. The people who have gathered on the street behind the yellow crime scene tape wear masks of shock and fear.

You can smell that fear in the street.

Police officers, firefighters, and paramedics alike wear their grief and sadness like a cloak. We've lost more of our own. Again. And this time not just one, but two.

All while eating a fucking hamburger.

I will probably never be able to stomach another one after today.

As I approach the yellow tape I hear someone call-ing my name. "Claire!" But I don't pay any attention. It's like I'm at the far end of a tunnel, and that tunnel is underwater. The voice is foggy or faint. It sounds so far away.,

"Claire!" it sounds again. "Get back!" But I keep walking towards the tape.

Each step I take feels as if it's encased in concrete. But I force myself to keep pushing forward. I have to see with my own two eyes before I can believe that this really happened. That our small township is under siege. But from who? From where? I don't know. I just don't know.

"God dammit, Lee!" the voice shouts again and I pause in my steps to look over my shoulder. Wes is running towards me from far away. "What the fuck is she doing here?"

I turn back towards my goal.

"She made me," Lee says to Wes.

"When does anyone make you do anything, Lee?" Wes roars. "God dammit, Lee, don't be such a pussy!"

"I swear it," Lee says.

"Dammit, Claire!" Wes shouts. "Get back!"

"No," I say. "I can't. I have to do this. I have to be here. For her."

"Please, baby. I'm begging you," he says. I look up and notice that Wes is right next to me although he doesn't make a move to pull me back. "Don't do it."

"I have to," I whisper. The look in his eyes is desolate. He knows I have to do this and he also knows it's not going to be good. Shit it must be bad. "Come with me?"

"Always," he vows to me.

"I want to be strong," I admit my voice low for Wes's ears only. "I don't want to fall apart before I have a chance to find who did this. Don't let me fall apart. Make me be strong."

"You *are* strong," Wes reassures me.

"Okay," I say for lack of anything else.

Wes wraps his arm around my waist and I let his strength seep into my bones. We approach the crime scene tape and I see the carnage for the first time. I feel the bile rise up in my throat, but I beat it back.

"She was eating a fucking hamburger on her dinner break," I say hearing the anger reverberate through my voice.

"Yes," he confirms the facts.

"A fucking hamburger." I grind my teeth together to keep from screaming.

"I know, honey," Wes says as he rubs my back. I dig my fingers into his hip.

"We're going to find the man who did this and we're going to make him pay," I say, my voice low.

"Yeah," Wes agrees. "We fucking are. And we're going to do it together."

"Okay." I take a deep breath for the first time this afternoon. "Where do we start?"

"Let's review everything that's visible from right here and then go forward from there," he orders. And I can do that.

I move my gaze towards the asphalt. "I see shell casings outside of the vehicle."

"Good," Wes says. "He stood outside the vehicle. That matches what we know from the distress call."

"There are one . . . two . . . three . . . four. I count four casings. That matches what we heard over the call," I confirm.

"It looks like Jasmine was down with one," he says

his voice soft. "Matt looks like a double tap. Emma will confirm."

"Yes," I say forcing myself to take another deep breath and look up. That's when I see it. "They're wearing body cams."

"It's standard practice now," Wes says before realizing what I'm saying.

"We need that footage," I tell him.

He turns to several other suits in the area. "I want this body cam footage yesterday!"

"Yes, Sir!" someone says as they jump to get him what he wants. Police and FBI alike will do anything to bring this guy down. We tend to band together when one of our own is murdered.

"Good work, Detective," he says.

"Thanks."

I watch Wes look around at all of the businesses on this street.

"I want all of the security footage from every shop or restaurant. Anyone who has one, get it!" Lee commands the officers.

I thought the scene on this street was bad until I heard the *pop . . .pop . . . pop* of a high velocity rifle report. After the mass shooting the other day, the entire law enforcement community responded to this shooting, the cold-blooded murder of two police officers while sitting in their squad car on their dinner break.

"It's a trap!" Lee shouts.

"Everyone take cover!" Wes yells over the roar of the blood in my ears.

We all dropped what we were doing a ran straight here in order to do our part to find justice for Jasmine and Matt. What we didn't know at the time was that it was a trap and we are all sitting ducks.

It's a sight to behold to watch the two of them take over as they issue commands to keep everyone safe. I can see how they worked so well together in their SEAL days.

"I want eyes on that building now!" Lee demands.

"He's gone, Captain," Officer Jones replies.

"Let's secure this scene and get the fuck out of here," Wes says.

"Captain the ME is here with her team and the body mover," Jones says.

"Abso-fucking-lutely not!" Lee yells. "She does not set foot in here until I have a three-click radius cleared. Do you hear me?"

"Copy that, Captain. Dr. Parker is going to be pissed though," Jones tells him, even though it's something we all already know.

"Let her be fucking pissed. Pissed is better than dead," Lee answers, his voice eerily calm.

"I hear that," Jones says before breaking out into a jog to tell Emma and her team that they have to sit and wait.

After what seems like forever, Emma and her team are finally allowed in when the area is secure, and the sniper is long gone. And as predicted, Emma is fuming mad.

"You don't get to make decisions for me and my team, Captain," she spits out my brother's title as if it's the most disgusting thing on the tip of her tongue.

"Yes, I fucking do," he snarls back. "I am the Captain of this department."

"And I don't fucking answer to you," she snarls.

"Yes, you do. This is my fucking crime scene," Lee practically growls. "And even if it wasn't I would never let you put yourself in harms way."

"Fortunately for you, I don't care about that either," she spits out.

"When are you going to cut me some fucking slack, Emma?" Lee asks as he runs a hand through his hair. "Can't you see that I care?"

"Can't you see that I don't?" she barks.

"If I believed that bullshit for a minute, I would walk away right now, but we both know that's not true, don't we?" he snaps.

"I don't know what you're implying?" she pouts but it's faked. The look on her face is worried and I can't help but stand here and watch them implode for the eightieth time this month.

"Don't you?" he asks taking a predatory step closer to her. Lowering his voice so only we can hear, Lee says, "You know that I love you like I know that you love me even though you like to pretend that you don't. Just like I know that tonight, like every other night, even though you don't want to admit that either, it'll be my cock that you ride and my name that you call out into the dark."

Emma audibly swallows past the lump in her throat.

"What's wrong, Angel? Cat got your tongue?" Lee presses into her personal space. They always seem to rise to the challenge with each other and never in a good way.

"I need to get to work," she says her voice unsteady and Emma, as a whole, appears to be off kilter. God they're a fucking mess. I wish they would just figure their shit out already but I'm not that lucky.

"That's what I thought," he replies, a smug expression playing on his face.

"We need to talk to some of these people to see if anyone say awything," Wes says effectively distracting me from the Lee and Emma show.

I look over my shoulder and see nervouse faces peering out of the windows from the small grocery store across the street. That is exactly where I am going to start.

"That's a great plan." I toss a thumb over my shoulder to indicate to Wes where exactly I am going to start questioning witnesses. "I'll be right over there."

Wes looks over to where I'm pointing. "Sounds like a plan. Keep me posted."

"Roger that." I awkwardly salute. It drives Wes nuts but he smirks. We both could use a little levity here in any form that it might come in.

I make my way over across the street to the small market which, for all intents and purposes, appears to be closed. And not just closed for today, but long term, maybe even indefinitley. The blinds are pulled and the lights are off but I know that there are people in here because I just saw them. Unless Casper the friendly ghost has taken up residence, these people must be scared.

I feel a hope, a thrill of excitement burn in my chest that I might just be on the right track because if these people are hiding like this, dollars to donuts, I would bet that they saw something they would rather forget.

I push the door open and it swings freely, the bells

on the door tinkling as they move with the door. I carefully step into the room and call out.

"Hello," I call out. "My name is Detective Goodnite and I would like to speak to anyone who might be in here."

"Go away!" someone shouts.

"I can't do that, Sir," I answer. "A friend of mine was murdered on this street this morning and I have to find out who did it."

"We didn't see anything," the man shouts again, hidden somewhere in the back. I stay rooted to my spot by the door as I answer him.

"I don't think that's quite true," I say gently. "Please help me."

"We have to help," a woman's heavily accented voice whispers harshly somewhere towards the back of the store.

"No!" the man whispers back.

"It is the right thing to do," she says and he sighs.

That trill of hope burns in my gut and blossoms in my chest. Thank God, I'm getting somewhere and this woman just scored a major point for me. An older couple shuffles out from behind one of the rows of shelves. They do not turn on any lights. I assume they are so scared that they don't want to attract any unwanted attention to themselves.

"We don't want any trouble," the man tells me confirming my suspicions.

"I don't want any trouble for you either," I say to him holding up my hands in front of me to show him that I mean in. "I just want to ask you some questions."

He looks to the woman stand ing next to him. The

way that she holds onto his arm and the familiar air they have about them tells me that she is his wife although neither one of them offer up that information. But it doesn't matter, right now that is not important.

She nods to him and he looks back at me. He lets out another sigh.

"We saw everything," he tells me. My palms start to sweat and I have to wipe them on my jeans.

"Please," I implore him. "Tell me everything."

"I'll start at the beginning," he says. "My wife and I open our store very early in the morning so we can take lunch together about noon every day. This lady cop and her partner buy lunch two, three times a week from Abraham down the street and eat there." He points out the window to across the street where Jasmine and Matt's carr still sits now littered with crime scene tape and evidence numbers.

"So you know Officer Alexander and Officer Jerome?" I ask him.

"Yes," he answers. "Jasmine is a nice girl. She's from around here. Her partner is not a nice man. *Was* not a nice man. May God have mercy on his soul."

"So then what happened?" ask him trying to get this train back on the tracks. And while it seemed no one liked Matt which is understanding because I personally always thought he was kind of an asshole, but still, by what I heard on the distress call earlier, it was Jasmine the killer targeted, *not Matt.*

"A man," he answers. "Walked right up to their car while we were sitting at the table here by the front windows and pulled a gun out from behind his back and shot our Jasmine and her partner."

"Can you describe him for me?" I ask pushing the words past the lump in my throat. I was right, they were murdered in cold blood while eating the hamburger that someone named Abraham sold them a couple of times a week. Anger burns in my gut.

"He was tall but not very," he answers vaguely. Come on, man, give me something, I think to myself. "Maybe six feet tall or there about. He had sandy blond hair and was on the thin side."

"No big muscles like the policeman you came here with," the wife adds describing the bulky muscle of my brother.

"And what was he wearing?" I ask them.

"A light blue polo shirt and jeans," the wife answers.

"Can you think of anything else?" I ask them.

"No," the wife says shaking her head.

"If you think of anything else," I say handing her my card. "Please call me."

"We don't want any trouble," the man says.

"I don't want any trouble for you either," I tell him before I step out of their small grocery store and back into the daylight.

After Emma and her team unload their supplies and begin to catalogue and collect every piece of evidence, Liam and Wes go back to directing the investigation. If anyone can track this mother fucker down, it's Liam and Wes. If he hadn't just murdered two good cops, I would almost feel sorry for him. But that's not the case. He took a bright light from this world and now? Now I will happily greet him at the gates of hell.

chapter 12

"LET'S GO HOME." By the time Wes tells me we're done for the day, the sun is going down, Emma had moved the bodies hours ago, and there is absolutely no evidence of the guy that murdered two police officers in cold blood.

I'm tired and frustrated. I'm hungry and sad. But most of all, I just want this nightmare to be over.

"We're done here for the night," Wes says as he reaches out to take my hand. I had been interviewing shopkeepers all afternoon but at this point I was just comforting them.

"If you think of anything else," I say to the older gentleman who owned the small grocery store. I hand him one of my cards. "Give me a call."

"I will," he says.

"Excuse me," I say politely as I let Wes lead me away.

We climb in his Fed-mobile without speaking a

word to each other. It's not that we're mad or upset with each other, in fact, just the opposite. But in moments like this, during cases like this, Wes and I both need a moment of quiet. The stillness helps me collect my thoughts and begin to process them. I have long believed that Wes operates in the same fashion.

Wes pulls into the driveway and we climb out of the car. He meets me at the hood with a scowl pulling between his brows. When we are at work, I am my own person, but when we're after hours, Wes likes to be a gentleman, opening doors for me and such. He gets frustrated when I don't let him. I grab his hands and squeeze his fingers gently, so he knows I didn't mean it as a slight to him.

He punches in the code and unlocks the front door, holding it open for me to pass through and I do. The house feels dark and ominous after the day that we have had so I switch on every light that I pass on my way to the kitchen and some that are out of my way too.

Wes trails behind me into the kitchen. He picks up the remote and starts clicking buttons while I pull last night's cold pizza out of the fridge. The screen lights up adding more false brightness to a dreary night.

"Hot or cold?" I ask but Wes isn't listening to me. He's turning up the volume on the television while I open the box.

I freeze when I hear the words coming out of the TV.

"This just in . . ." the female news anchor says. "Station KVXY has received an anonymous note that we believe to be from the killer . . ."

"That's correct, Marcy . . ." the male anchor says. *"This station received a letter late this afternoon. As you all know, we have been covering the case of the police murders since mid-day . . ."*

"That is correct, Steve," she says as she turns her smile to him. I hate her. She's annoying, she wants Wes, and someone invited her to our wedding, but in this moment, I hate her most of all. *"We are going to read that letter to you now."*

"The letter reads as follows," Steve the news anchor says holding up a sheet of white paper.

"That better not be the actual note," Wes growls as he pulls out his phone and starts texting someone—probably either Lee or someone in his own chain of command—while watching the news. My eyes are glued to the screen and I can't make myself look away. "So much for fucking evidence."

" 'Dear Citizens of George Washington Township and the surrounding areas, You have probably noticed some events of recent are not the usual for our sleepy little township. I can assure you that they will eventually stop and the place we call home will be safe once again. But not quite yet. You see someone has to pay for their transgressions . . ."

Oh God, I feel the bile rise up in my throat. I don't know who this guy is, but I have a sinking feeling what's coming. My luck has held steady at bad all year and it can't have magically flipped the dial to good all of a sudden.

"Detective Claire Goodnite has been a very bad girl and until she is willing to right those wrongs . . ."

"What the actual fuck?!" Wes roars.

"Wes," I whimper.

"The shooting last week and the one today were all my handiwork. And such events will continue until I have the apology that I so rightly deserve. Until then . . .'" the news anchor reads. *"And it's signed 'The Hunter.'"*

"I don't like this at fucking all," Wes snaps.

"I-I . . ." I start but I don't know how to finish it. I don't know what words should come out of my mouth. But most importantly, I don't know what I have done or to who that would cause this kind of retaliation.

Wes's phone rings and he pulls it back out of his pocket having only placed it there moments before.

"Yeah?" he answers. "We saw it . . . Not good, brother . . . right . . ." and then he hangs up.

My whole body is shaking. I'm not hungry and I don't know what to do. Wes pockets his phone and opens his mouth to tell me what whoever that was on the other end of the phone, probably my brother, had to say but when he looks at me and sees my face—what has to be the terror that I'm feeling telegraphed across my face—and the way that my body shakes he turns to me quickly. His legs eating up the ground between us in quick strides.

"Claire, fuck, baby," he starts but I don't have anything to say. "Come here."

Wes pulls me into his arms and holds me tight but even he can't stop the shaking that quakes my body. He lifts me up into his arms and carries me upstairs to our bedroom.

"What do you need, baby?" he asks me when he sets me back on my feet.

"I d-d-don't know," I answer, and I don't. I have no idea what could right what is so obviously wrong in my life right now.

"A shower? Tea? Bed?" he asks as I shake my head no. Nothing sounds good right now.

"Shower," I answer. "I have to scrub clean."

"Okay," Wes says as he marches us into the bathroom.

He flips on the lights before turning on the shower to heat up. Wes backs out of the shower and begins stripping off our clothes but what is usually fun, and seduction is replaced with economical movements that serve a purpose.

When we're both naked, he takes my hand and pulls me into the shower stall and directly under the steaming water. I let the scalding spray sting my skin in hopes that I will snap out of what has me twisted in knots so that I can make heads or tails of what is going on.

Wes pulls a bottle of shampoo off of the shelf and pours some in his hands before massaging it into my hair. He tips my head back under the spray and rinses the suds out gently like you would a child.

He hands me the tube of my face soap to wash up as he quickly showers himself clean and I scrub my face until it feels raw, but I still don't feel clean. The way Wes looks at me with concern in his eyes says I might have actually scrubbed my skin raw.

Wes picks up a bar of soap that he just scrubbed his body with and carefully washes every inch of my skin, but not in the harsh way that I had just washed my face. He rinses the soap from my skin and shuts off the taps, grabbing a towel as he steps out. He dries his body quickly before touching the soft terry cloth to my skin chasing the droplets away.

"What do you need, baby?" he asks me. "Food?"

"No," I answer honestly. I couldn't eat even if I wanted to.

"Bed?" he asks. That's probably the only thing that I can handle. I need to sleep the rest of this day away. I only hope that when I close my eyes, it's not Jasmine and Matt's lifeless bodies that I see.

"Bed."

"You got it," he says as he walks me over the bed and pulls the blanket and sheet back for me to climb in.

Wes climbs in behind me and pulls the covers over us cocooning us from the outside world. But it's when he pulls me into his arms that I bury my face in his chest and finally lose it.

"I-i-i-it's all my fault," I cry.

"No, baby, it's not," he tells me but, in my head, over and over again, I hear that bitch on the news tell me that it is.

"It is!" I sob. "He said so."

"This is the working of a madman," Wes says quietly just letting me cry. "Normal people don't go on shooting rampages because they are mad about some transgression."

"But he blames me!" The tears are flowing free down my cheeks and I can't seem to catch my breath.

"Claire—" Wes starts but I don't let him finish.

"Rodriguez and Matt are dead because of me," I sob. "Jasmine is dead because of me!"

Wes wisely does not interrupt my meltdown, he

just holds me through the storm. And while what he said is true, only madmen harm others as punishments for whatever slights they perceive happened, but that fact of the matter is, this guy blames me—not anyone else but me.

When my tears have run dry and the sobs that wrack my chest are echoes of the ones that came before them, I finally close my eyes. My fingers still clinging to Wes as he holds me, and I succumb to my exhaustion and fall into sleep.

Run!

I'm running as fast as my little feet will take me through the woods behind my parents' house. I have to get away from the bad man. If he catches me now, I'll never get away. I have to be free.

Run! I have to run faster.

I see the blue gray light as it spills through the trees. Mommy always told me this was her favorite part of the day—looking at the sun as it comes up in the morning. I ran away late in the night. I had to wait until he came for me one more time. When he unlocks the closet door, I'm ready, I have the baseball bat I found in the back of the closet. When he opens the door, I hit him with it and run, dropping the bat in my tracks.

Free.

I'm free. That's the words in my head as the tree break and I see Wes standing at the edge of the back-

yard. I'm free. I'm finally free. Wes looks up and he sees me.

"I've got her!" he shouts to someone.

My heart is beating so hard in my chest and it hurts to breathe. I'm so tired but I have to keep running. I see Wes, his face, I know that he'll protect me. Wes always protects me. He will keep me safe. He will keep me free.

I push my feet just a little harder, I run just a little faster. I'm almost there. But when I push through the trees, Wes isn't reaching for me. He is standing over a pile of bodies—the bodies of Officer Rodriguez, Officer Jerome, and Officer Alexander. Their mangled corpses are littered at his feet.

When Wes finally turns to me his face is not full of hope and of love for me, but one of anger and disgust. I know in that moment that Wes hates me even before he opens his mouth to talk.

"This is all your fault, Claire."

"No!" I scream. It's not my fault but in my heart of hearts, I know that it really is. "No! Don't hate me, please."

"Claire," someone says my name.

"Don't hate me! I need you," I beg.

"Claire, baby," someone says as they shake me awake.

"Please! I'm so sorry. I didn't mean to!" I wail.

"God dammit! Wake up, Claire!" Wes roars and I gasp as I come fully awake.

The realization that it was another nightmare has

rocked me.

"Wes," I plead.

"I'm right here, baby," he reassures me.

I push up out of the bed. I have to move. My body is restless, and I don't know what to do other than to pace but Wes has other ideas.

"What's wrong?" he asks me as he hauls me back into the bed and back against his body.

"I have to move!" I shout. "Let me go! Can't you see I have to move?"

"You're restless?" he asks. "Your nightmare rattled you and you're restless."

"Yes," I say through gritted teeth.

"Tell me about it," he demands.

"No, please," I plead.

"Get it out," Wes orders. "It's a poison and you have to cut it out."

"Yes," I agree before I begin to explain. "I was running. I had escaped, and I could see you through the trees in the clearing. You saw me . . ."

"Yes, that happened," he tells me. "What else?"

"But when I got there you weren't reaching for me." He frowns at me looking confused. This is clearly the part of the story that goes off script. "When I get there the bodies of all the cops are at your feet and when you look at me I know that you hate me."

"Claire—" he tries to interrupt but I don't let him. He is right. The truth is like a poison and I have to get it out.

"You tell me that it's all my fault and it is!" I shout into the dark room.

"No." He shakes his head vehemently.

"It is!" I argue. "Now do you see why I can't sit still? That I have to move?"

"Run or fuck?" he asks me.

"What?"

"You said that you need to move," he explains. "So, we'll do it together. Do you want to run or fuck?" It only takes me a minute to decide.

"Fuck."

"Hard and fast. That's the only way to fight out what you need to," he tells me.

"Yes." I feel my body heating against his.

"It won't be sweet."

"No," I tell him. "I don't want that."

Wes nods once before rolling me to my back and sliding in hard and fast at the same time. I cling to his back, my nails digging in as he pumps into my body hard and fast, just as he had promised me.

It is not sweet and loving nor is it romantic and meaningful. It's sweaty and dirty, it's teeth and nails, and it's exactly what I needed in the moment.

After my orgasm washes through me I finally feel a glimmer of the calm that I had been craving. Wes holds me, his cock still deep inside me as the sweat cools and we can finally catch our breath.

"I can't be without you, Wes," I say softly before the moment is over and I lose my chance to speak my feelings and my fears.

"You won't, baby."

"You can't promise me that, Wes," I sigh. "We don't know what the future will hold."

"I can," he says his voice ringing strong and true in the bedroom.

"How?" I ask my voice sounding small and unsure but, in this moment,, I will take whatever reassurances that Wes can give me.

"Because I'm just that fucking good," he says. "Can you sleep now?"

"Yeah, I think I can," I tell him.

"Alright, honey," he says as he rolls and curls me into him, settling us back into the bed.

As I drift off again the wisps of calm in the storm that Wes had given me start to drift away and I'm left with the gut deep feeling that nothing will ever be okay again. And in a few short days, I would come to realize how very right I was . . .

chapter 13

officially official

"I NEED YOU ON this case," Lee says to me when I walk into his office the next morning.

When Wes and I had gotten up this morning we were more somber than usual. There was nothing about this morning that called for our usual morning hanky panky, so we quietly showered, dressed, and then he drove me to the station.

Wes had kissed me softly on the lips with a quiet, "I'll see you later." And then he was gone.

I had walked to my desk and fired up my computer so that I could go over everything I knew about both shootings. I was lost in case notes when my brother had called me into his office with a hollered "Goodnite!"

That was ten minutes ago and now Lee had just said that he needed me on this case. For years I have been waiting for him to say those very words. Years!

"What was that?" I ask feeling a little petty.

"The department needs all hands-on deck for this asshole. As much as I hate to admit it, you're the best."

Lee sighs and runs a hand through his hair. A gesture I have come to know as one of frustration.

"Awe, thanks big brother." I smile an I-just-won-Ms.-America smile.

"Yeah . . . well, don't get used to it," Lee barks.

"Sure thing, boss." I wink at him

"I'm setting up a task force. Say hello to you new partner," Lee explains to me. I had a feeling who I would see before I even turned around.

"Hey, Fed. What's up?" I ask on another wink. Fake good humor can take a gal a long way. Fake it till you make it and all that . . .

"That's Special Agent O'Connell to you." He winks at me.

"Yes, Special Agent O'Connell." I mock salute. "Yeah, I'm not sure how I feel about that."

"We'll try it again tonight when I pull your hair and fuck you from behind," he rumbles for my ears only. Forgetting for a moment that we were in Lee's office. Whoops.

"That does hold some merit."

"Yeah, I'm going to need the assurance of a little decorum in front of the rest of the task force…"

"Aye aye, Captain," I say. Lee sighs.

"You two are officially investigating the Hunter case," he says. Gone is the joking and ridiculousness. This case calls for nothing but seriousness and focus.

"You got it," I tell him.

"Yeah, I think that I do," Lee says softly after giving me an appraising look. "See that I don't regret this."

"You won't.

"You need to prepare a press conference," Lee orders.

"Roger that," Wes says.

"Keep me in the loop," Lee tells us. "Now get out of my office."

As Wes and I head out of Lee's office my cell phone chimes from my back pocket.

"Goodnite," I answer.

"Hey, it's me," Emma says. "Come down to my lair." And then she hangs up.

"What was that?" Wes asks me.

"We've been summoned to Emma's domain," I explain on a shrug.

"Well then let's hop to it." Wes claps his hands.

We follow the path through the bullpen to the elevator and I lean forward and push the call button. Wes and I stand side by side as we wait for the elevator to take us down to the basement morgue that Emma calls her home away from home.

The bell chimes as the steel doors slide open and Wes follows me into the metal box. He pushes the button for the bottom and we ride down.

"What the hell took you so long?" Emma shouts when the doors slide open.

"The elevator?" I droll.

"Funny, funny," she snaps before turning to Wes. "What's shaking hot Fed?"

"A task force to find the Hunter," he explains.

"I heard about that," she says as she looks me over. I can't help but feel like these two see all of my secrets on the surface. "How are you doing?"

"About as good as expected," I answer.

"So not actually good at all," Emma reads between

the lines.

"Exactly."

"So, what do you have?" Wes effectively changes the subject.

"My buddy ballistics," she answers on a bright smile. Emma is kind of an odd duck. "The same high velocity rifle was used in both shootings."

"What was it?" I ask.

"Looks to be a Springfield, smooth bore thirty-ot-six," she answers.

"Registered?" Wes asks.

"Nope." She pops the p sound which always drives me bonkers mad.

"It was probably bought in pieces and assembled at home," I say thinking allowed.

"That's true," Wes agrees.

"Now here's where things get interesting," Emma begins. "Jerome and Alexander were done with a forty-five at close range. That doesn't fit the mass shooting profile."

"That was the bait," I say. "To get us all there so that he could shoot at us."

"I thought so too," she says. "But after last night's news broadcast, I can't help but wonder if it was more personal since you and Jasmine were friends."

"If that's the case," Wes says. "Then you better watch your back, Emma."

"My thoughts exactly, Fed-Man."

"You got anything else for us?" I ask Emma.

"That was it," she says. "Watch your back, sister. The enemy is close."

"You too," I say softly. Emma winks at me just before Wes and I turn for the elevator.

"Let's go show those reporters who's boss." Wes winks at me as we climb into the elevator.

"And which reporters do you suppose will be at this press conference?" I ask as casually as I can. Wes rolls his eyes telling me that he's onto my ulterior motives.

"You know that Marcy and Steve will be there. They broke the story and they will want to follow it through," he tells me with his voice soft and thoughtful. I absolutely hate it.

"Yippee," I say without the enthusiasm the word implies.

"Claire," Wes chastises. "Be nice."

"It's hard to be nice when every time she sees you she's practically humping your leg," I complain.

"She does not." Wes looks me in the eye with all seriousness and I just stare right back.

"She does too."

"Okay, she does but that's not the point. I'm with you," he says to me.

"You better be with me or they will never find your body," I growl under my breath. Wes just throws his head back and laughs before crowding me into the corner of the elevator.

"Baby, you know that I am exactly where I want to be, or I wouldn't be here," Wes says, his voice low and full of sex and something more. "I did not just chase you for years. Years, Claire! Watching you with other guys, waiting for you to clue in that I was here and waiting. Only to finally get my ring on your finger and your glorious ass in my bed every night only to turn around and chase after someone like Marcy."

"Well," I say for lack of anything better.

"Years, Claire." He sighs running his hand through his hair. "I'm not going anywhere."

"Okay," I say softly. "You're mine and you aren't going anywhere. Well, I have news for you buddy, neither am I."

"Now, you should probably push the button if you want this elevator to actually go anywhere. Or we could take the stairs. Your call, baby. But whichever you choose, I'll be right behind you."

I roll my eyes and push the button in the elevator to the tune of Wes's low laughter.

"Ugh, fine," I groan as I push the button in the elevator. "Let's go show everyone how officially official we are so that we can catch this asshole and solve the damn case."

"And then we'll get married."

"Yes, Wes." I sigh. He's lucky I find him cute when he's persistent. "Then we'll get married."

Silently I add the *I hope* to the end. One thing I would learn in the coming days was that hope was all we had left and even that was about to be sorely tested

. . .

chapter 14

SPECIAL TASK FORCE, *my ass. Who do they think they are dealing with? I am clearly the superior competitor and they never stood a chance. They will never catch me before I catch them I think it's time I left them a little reminder.*

When is she going to learn? While I find myself becoming frustrated with Claire I have to remind myself that she will be so much fun when I bring her to heel. That is what I have been waiting for all this time. What I have been working for.

She needs to learn that she chose wrong. All of this is on her head, not mine. The blood spilled is on Claire's hands, I am just the tool with which to serve her punishment.

And soon I will be the master of her universe when I bring her world crumbling down. Yes, my queen needs to learn to kneel at the feet of her king and beg for mercy. Of which I am not sure I will give.

But first I have to send my queen a message . . .

"Do you feel Detective Goodnite is fit for duty?"

That question came about ten minutes after Wes and I walked into the press room at the station on the heels of Liam to answer questions about the Hunter case. And that disgusting question came dripping from none other than the over inflated lips of Marcy the news anchor. Yay!

"Good afternoon ladies and gentlemen of the press. My name is Liam Goodnite and I am the Captain of this department," Lee said when he walked up to the podium.

"Is this about the Hunter case?" Marcy asked.

"Yes, it is," he confirmed.

"I would be happy to work Agent O'Connell," she said, her voice full of victory. God, I hate her. "The Hunter reached out to me, after all."

"The Hunter allegedly reached out to the news station KVXY," Lee said. "We have yet to confirm it."

"Don't be ridiculous," she snapped. "I have proof."

"I will be needing all evidence turned over to the joint task force between the George Washington Township PD and the FBI. They are now tasked with bringing this killer to justice."

"I will be happy to turn them over to Special Agent O'Connell personally," she had purred.

As much as I love Wes in this moment—and I know that he meant well—but here is where he fucked up. "You can turn them over to my partner on the joint task force, Detective Goodnite."

"Do you feel Detective Goodnite is fit for duty?" she asks now as I stand here a little dumbfounded that this press conference went downhill so fast.

"I do," Wes confirms.

"You can't mean that," Marcy snapped.

"I do," Wes repeats.

"Could that be because she offers you special perks to the job?" Marcy asks, her voice turning vicious.

"If you're referring to the fact that Detective Goodnite and I are engaged to be married, then yes, we are. However, as we are professionals in our field we are able to separate our work lives from our home lives," Wes warns.

"Engaged?" she gasps.

"Yes," I answer holding up the back side of my hand to show off my glittering ring. "Now if we could get back to the task force . . ."

"Excellent idea, Detective Goodnite," Lee says.

"Captain Goodnite, don't you think it's a conflict of interest to have Detective Goodnite on this task force?"

"No," he says his voice firm.

"But the Hunter made it clear that this is all her fault."

I don't move my mouth, but I do gasp. Her words sting. I know that I blame myself and the Hunter definitely blames me but for other people to blame me hurts. I feel the burn of my own shame creep across my face.

"That is ridiculous," Wes snaps. "Only a madman

blames his cruel actions on someone else. Detective Goodnite has never been responsible for this person."

"I'm just saying," Marcy starts. "That there is no place for her here."

"Detective Goodnite was born in George Washington Township and has worked in one capacity or another for the department for over ten years. If anyone has a place here, it's her," says Lee making me smile. "I think that's about all we have time for today, folks. Marcy, I expect you to turn over all evidence in your possession or I will get a court order."

"Then get a court order," she snarls. "I'm not giving her shit."

"I could arrest you for obstructing justice," Lee warns.

"Go ahead and try," she snaps back. "That is unless, it's Agent O'Connell with the handcuffs . . . then I'm available."

"Don't count on it," I say under my breath.

"You know your mom called me last week and offered to give me your number, but I told her that I already had it. Come on, Wes, you know how good we are together. How . . . electric."

I think I'm going to hurl.

"That's enough, Marcy," Wes warns.

"Call me when you get bored of her. I know how to keep you happy." She winks and then she's out the door.

"Claire—" Wes starts but I just hold out my palm to silence him.

"I'm not judging you by your past lovers . . . but yeah, I'm judging you by your past lovers." I force out a sigh barely holding in a laugh. "Thank God you found me when you did." I finally laugh. Wes and Lee join in too.

"I thank God every day I found you."

chapter 15

call it in

"**READY TO GET OUT** of here?" Wes asks me after we wrapped up the press conference that was an epic shit show and closed up shop for the night.

"Yeah," I let out a sigh.

"I'll catch you kids later," Lee says as he palms his keys and heads for the rear door of the station.

"You know he's going to go see Emma, right?" I ask Wes.

"Claire," Wes says, his voice full of warning. "Stay out of it."

"I think it's time we stop lying to each other, Wes, and start this marriage with honesty, don't you?" I ask him.

"Yes . . ." he says hesitantly.

"I agree," I say on a nod. "So, let's be real here. I think we both know I'm not going to stay out of it so I'm going to stop pretending like I will."

Wes laughs. "You are ridiculous sometimes, you know that?" he asks me.

"But I'm your ridiculous and that's really what's important here."

"Yeah, baby," he says on a smile. "You are."

Wes takes my hand in his and walks me out of the station. He beeps the locks on his Fed-mobile and opens the passenger door for me. This car is truly ridiculous. Even if I didn't know he was a federal agent, the dark maroon Crown Vic with government plates sure cleared that up for me.

"Don't look at me like that," Wes laughs.

"Like what?" I ask.

"Like you're silently judging my company wheels," he elaborates.

"Oh yeah, I totally am." I laugh.

"I know you are," Wes says as he drives us through town.

I hate this part of cases like this. Where you hurry up and wait. There is no quick moving casework, there are no miraculous discoveries like you see on TV. Real police work is slow moving. The cases don't magically solve themselves and it takes sheer will and determination to find that tiny little needle in a haystack to solve them most times.

This is one of those cases.

So, while we've had busy days it feels like we're getting nowhere fast and I hate it. It drives me crazy especially when it's someone like Jasmine. I want to solve every case, but it sticks in my craw when it's such a heartless crime in cold blood. For Christ's sake she was eating a fucking hamburger. It wasn't even a fair fight.

My mind is wandering when Wes finally pulls into

our driveway, otherwise I would have noticed the surprise waiting for me.

"Call it in," Wes snaps gathering my attention.

"Call what in?" I ask as I look up. "Oh."

"Yeah, 'oh.'" He bites out a curse.

Painted across the garage door—which was a really nice one that was made to look like an old carriage door and I really liked it—in blood red paint, which really, is not very original is "This is all your fault, Claire."

I sigh. "I really hate surprises."

"Yeah," Wes says. "When it comes to you and this house, I really hate surprises too."

"Hey," I rally. "Look on the bright side, it's not a snake."

"Not funny, Claire," Wes warns.

"What?" I ask feigning my innocence.

"You know what? Never mind." He sighs running his hand through his brown hair. "I have to call this in."

"I'll call Lee," I offer. "You call in the Feds."

"Claire . . ." Wes shoots me a side eye glare.

"What?" I ask again.

"Can you even say 'FBI'?" he asks me.

"No, it's tastes funny on my tongue," I say making a face.

"You know the FBI pays for this house you live in," he informs me.

"Whatever." I roll my eyes making Wes smile. Damn, I love his smile. It always makes me feel better when I'm down and still manages to give me butterflies. "I could always go back to my old apartment . . ."

"The hell you could," he barks.

"That's what I thought," I mumble feeling a little smug.

"Just call Lee, would you?" he sighs. "And the get your ass inside before we get shot by a raving lunatic."

"Okay," I mumble. "So touchy."

"I can hear you!" he shouts.

"I'm calling Lee now," I say loudly as I fish my phone out of my pocket and dial my brother as we head into the house. "I'm not talking to you."

It rings three times . . . four . . . Jesus, Lee. This is fucking important. Five rings . . . Wes is talking to his office and I'm feeling a little like a dickwad standing here calling my brother only to have it ring six . . . no, seven times before he finally answers sounding a little out of breath.

"What could you possibly want right now?" he *barks into his phone.*

"Wow, good talking to you too, asshole. Never fucking mind," I snap feeling a little irritated and under loved.

He sighs. "I'm sorry, was it important?" he *asks me.*

"No, not at all," I reply blandly.

"Good tell me about it in the morning," he says.

"Nah," I say wanting to reach into the phone and slap the shit out of my brother for preferring to get laid instead of answering the phone when I have a goddamned emergency. "I'll just tell the FBI agents when they get here. Have a nice night!"

"Wait! Claire—" he shouts but I hang up. He might call back or maybe even show up, but he deserves this for being an asshole. Am I acting like a child right

now? Yes. Will I take it back? Hell no.

I see the red and blue lights heading up the hill towards the house from the front window and I let out a weary sigh. Wes moves to stand next to me and puts his arm around me in a mix of protecting and comforting and I greatly appreciate it.

"Did you get ahold of Lee?" he asks me.

"Something like that," I say.

"Uh-oh. What happened?"

"He's an asshole and said I should call him in the morning to tell him whatever was bothering me," I explain.

"What?!" Wes roars. "You did tell him what happened, right?"

"Well, he didn't really give me a chance, so I just hung up on him. He sounded . . . preoccupied."

Wes hangs his head. "Really?"

"Kind of . . . out of breath," I say. I have to bite my lip to keep from laughing at the scenario, at the look on Wes's face right now, at everything.

"I kind of want to say 'way to go, buddy.' Then again I kind of want to punch his face in," Wes says on a sigh. "I'm so torn."

"I know. Me too," I agree whole-heartedly.

Wes and I step back out onto the front porch when a couple of black and white's and a couple of Fed-mobiles pull up to block the driveway and the curb in front of the house. Jones steps out of the first car and shakes his head when he sees me.

"We really have to stop meeting like this, Goody," he laughs.

"Hey, at least it's not a snake," I say in good humor

trying my luck at my joke one more time.

"Claire—" Jones starts.

"What?" I ask. "Too soon?"

"Just a little," he laughs.

"That's what I said!" Wes joins in.

"I guess everyone's a critic tonight!" I harrumph.

"So, what do we have here?" one of the Feds asks.

"Someone painted a lovely note for my wife-to-be on our garage door—" Wes starts.

"I loved that garage door," I pout. "Why would someone do that?"

"Maybe because they are a deranged sociopath?" Wes asks.

"That's probably true," I agree with him.

"May I proceed?" he asks.

"Yes," I smile sweetly at him. "You may."

"Thank you," Wes says to me before moving on. "As you can see, we saw it when we pulled into the driveway this evening."

"Has anything been moved or touched?" the Fed asks. I narrow my eyes. This isn't my first rodeo. Wes squeezes my hip, so I stay quiet.

"No," he answers. "We called it in as soon as we could." That was mostly true.

"Let's get Crime Scene in here," the agent shouts to the group when Lee pulls up to the curb looking worse for the wear.

Lee and Emma—also looking pretty bedraggled— jump out of Lee's Tahoe and I'm feeling pretty pleased by the sight of them so unkept.

"Don't—" Wes starts.

"Well, I guess we know who Lee was entertaining," I mumble.

"Comment," he finishes.

"Too late."

"I see that." Wes sighs. His lot in life is really rough sometimes.

"What the hell is going on here?" Lee roars.

"Well so nice of you to finally make it, Captain," Jones smirks. "Dr. Parker."

"Shut it," Lee snaps. "Will someone tell me why I am just now finding out that one of my officers was threatened by the Hunter?"

"I'm thinking you don't want to open this line of dialogue right now, brother," Wes says subtly.

"Oh, I think I do."

"It's your funeral," Wes shrugs like it's not sweat off of his back.

"Maybe if you weren't so busy thinking with your dick you would know that when I called you an hour ago, I was trying to tell you about this," I snap. "But instead I was told to report to your office in the morning. So, you can either pitch in and figure this out so I can go to bed or you can get your happy ass back in your truck and go home."

"Claire—" Emma starts.

"You decide," I order not taking my eyes off of my wayward brother.

"Agent Cortez," he says breaking eye contact. "Tell me what we've got."

And just like that, my brother decides to be a grown up. Well how about that?

chapter 16

missing something

BY THE TIME THE Crime Scene unit rolls out Wes and I are beyond exhausted.

I have big plans to climb the stairs and flop into bed. Hopefully, all of this happens before I fall asleep. Wes, on the other hand, has other plans.

He shuts and locks the door behind us before he scoops me up in his arms like a bride and carries me up the stairs. Wes takes his time, he's not in any hurry because he knows that I am right where I want to be—held in his arms like I am all that truly matters in the world. I put my head on his shoulder and relax.

When we reach our bedroom, Wes sets me on my feet while he pulls his side arm and holster from his shoulder. I pull mine from my waist and boot, handing them to him to lock up for the night.

I stand there patiently and wait for him to return from the closet. Wes doesn't keep me waiting long. When he returns to me he is wearing his suit pants and belt, but he lost his button-down shirt and government issued tie in the closet along with his shoes and socks. The sight of his bare feet always did do me in.

Wes steps up behind me and pulls my t-shirt over my head letting it fall to the floor. My breath catches in my throat when he places a soft kiss to my bare shoulder as he unhooks my bra. I let the ribbon and lace fall to the floor. Wes cups my breasts in his palms and I lean back against his bare chest.

His thumbs skate over my nipples as he nibbles at the spot between my shoulder and my neck and I am gone. Wes glides one heavy palm down my belly to the front of my jeans where pops the button and pulls down the zipper one handed.

"Wes," I gasp when he slides that hand down the front of my jeans and under my panties.

His fingertips immediately find my entrance. Wes swirls his fingertip through my wetness before bringing it up to circle my clit over and over again.

I whimper at the loss of his fingers when he pulls them free from my pussy and then shoves my jeans and panties down my legs. I step out of them and kick them away.

Wes takes my hand and leads me over to the bed. I lay back into the middle of the bed as Wes follows me down. He covers me with his body, his mouth on mine but it's soft and sweet—not harsh and desperate.

When he slides into my body it's like coming home. Wes is my home. He brings me back to center when I feel lost and out of control. He is my North Star that guides me home in the dark and I should have known all along. I can live without him, but now that I have lived with him, I don't even want to try.

Wes pumps his cock into my waiting body and my climax washes over me like waves in the ocean, not all consuming and out of control but steady waves, one after the other. He drinks in my moans and whimpers as he places soft kisses of the corners of my mouth and my eyes, my cheeks and my chin.

And then finally, when the last of the waves crashes and I begin to surface, only then does Wes plant himself to the root and come inside me.

"I love you so much," he says softly.

"I love you too, Wes."

He rolls us to the side and holds me as we fall asleep.

It's dark. So dark.

At night my mommy leaves a nightlight on for me and my favorite piggy stuffed animal that I've had for ages to help me sleep. I hate the dark. Monsters only lurk in the dark. I want my mommy, but I can't cry. If I cry, the bad man will come and he will hurt me again. He always hurts me. Even though I don't want him to, I know, he always comes, but this time I will be ready.

I was digging in the closet when I knew that he was asleep. I found a pile of old junk. He must have been too lazy to clean out the closet that has been my prison for I don't know how long. But his laziness is my win. In the corner under the pile of old stuff, I found a baseball and then a glove, and in the very bottom of the pile, I found an old metal bat. Just like the kind Liam and Wes used when they were my age.

Sometimes it pays to be the little sister. My whole life I've been following Wes and Liam around hoping that they would play with me. I even told Wes that one day he would marry me. He just laughed and said, "I'm not so sure about that, Squirt." That's what he calls me. Squirt.

So, all the times, I followed them around when they played ball or walked in the woods finally is going to pay off even if Wes never wants to marry me because I learned how to swing a baseball bat watching them. I learned to run through the woods following them. I am going to run away from the bad man because of everything that I watched them do.

So, I wait. And I wait, and I wait, and I wait. I almost fall asleep. Almost. I feel my eyelids getting heavy but then I hear footsteps and I know that he's coming. He always comes.

I sit quietly and try not to make any noise. I hurry to my feet and grab my bat. I crouch in the corner with the bat over my shoulder just like Liam showed me how to do. When I hear the lock that he keeps on the closet door open I know that it's time.

My hands sweat, and I feel shaky all over.

"Wake up, Claire, it's time," he says as he pulls open the closet door. "What are you doing?" He asks when he sees me, but I don't answer. I swing the bat as hard as I can, hitting him in his big belly.

When the bad man falls forward, I swing one more time, hitting the side of his head just like Liam and Wes taught me to hit a baseball when I finally got them to include me. And then I run.

"Claire!" he shouts. "You better get back here right this minute."

I run out of the closet while the bad man screams my name. I run out of the ugly house that smells funny and then I run out into the woods.

I run, and I run, and I run. But I know he's going to catch me. A mean hand grabs me by my arm from behind and I scream . . .

I scream.

I scream, and I scream, and I scream. I try to shake off the hand that has me, but his grip is too strong. He is too strong.

"Claire, baby, wake up," Wes says as he shakes my arm. "Baby, it's me."

"Wes?" I ask.

"Yeah, honey," he says softly.

"I'm okay," I say trying to reassure myself.

"You're okay," Wes tells me.

I sit up in bed and the sheets stick to my sweaty skin. My stomach pitches back and forth and my head is pounding. I bring my knees up to my chest and rest my forehead on them while I try and catch my breath.

Wes sits up in the bed next to me letting the sheets pool around his trim hips. He puts his arm around me just holding me. Offering me comfort but not seeking or demanding anything from me. God, I love this man.

"So, you want to talk about it?" he asks me. Wes's

whiskey smooth voice sounds in the dark room.

"I think . . ." I begin and then tail off.

"Yeah, baby?" Wes asks me.

"I think that I'm missing something," I admit.

"You're missing something in your memories or in the Hunter case?" Wes asks me.

"Both," I answer.

"Okay," he says softly. "What do we need to do to figure it out?" And I love that. He is not telling me that I need to figure it out or demanding that I move on, but instead, Wes is asking me what we can do together because we are a team. Wes and I are a we, not a me or a him, but a we. Together we can figure it all out. I hope.

"I don't know yet," I admit.

"Well, when you do, let me know, okay?"

"Okay," I tell him.

I only hope that when I figure it all out that it won't be too late.

Famous last words . . .

chapter 17

sitting duck

B*EEP . . . BEEP . . . BEEP . . .*

When Wes's alarm sounds in the morning I'm both groggy and restless. My lack of sleep from the night before has me fuzzy and feeling like my head is full of cotton and my eyes are gritty and full of sand.

But it is the overwhelming feeling that I am missing something vital that has me throwing the sheets back and leaping out of bed on the second beep of Wes's phone.

All night long I tossed and turned after talking my nightmare out with Wes. I can't help but feel like maybe it really is all my fault. I know that sounds crazy, but at this point, I have to look at every angle and for whatever reason, this guy has decided to focus on me. I can't say that I'm thrilled about that but if it gets me the answers that I need then who cares.

It's a sacrifice that I am more than willing to make. But the lives of my officers are most definitely not.

"Where's the fire, babe?" Wes asks as I'm halfway

across the floor to the closet already.

"The station!" I shout over my shoulder. "I'm missing something. I just know it!"

I pull a bra and panties from my drawers at random and haphazardly pull them on my body not caring if they match or not. I grab a t-shirt and pull it over my head when Wes follows me into the closet and starts donning his Fed suit. I have to admit that it's an interesting progression from every day guy to super fed.

"I know," he tells me as he wraps his tie around his neck. "I know we're missing something too, but what?"

"I don't know," I answer as I pull on my jeans.

"For whatever reason," Wes says as he pulls on his dress shoes. "He's fixated on you."

"I know." I pull on my sneakers and drop a pancake holster into the back of my pants instead of my usual side holster. Today I feel the need to be invisible.

"Who would have a beef with you?" Wes asks me as he pulls his shoulder holster on.

"Other than Marcy?" I ask.

"Babe, you have to let Marcy go." He rolls his eyes.

"I know."

Wes grabs our side arms out of the safe and hands me mine. I drop my badge in my pocket along with my phone.

"Also, we know that the Hunter is a man," Wes adds. "And as much as I hate to ask this, but I have to. Any scorned lovers in your past?"

"No," I answer right away. "I barely stopped to collect a first name. I didn't actually date anyone."

"The thought of you with any other man makes me

want to vomit," Wes says looking a little green around the gills.

"Well, we couldn't all be as discerning as you were in your single days . . ." I roll my eyes.

"You know I wasn't a monk while I was waiting for you to either grow up or give me the time of day, babe."

"I know," I sigh. "But now you know how I feel about all of the Marcys of the world that pop up and flaunt their extensive knowledge of your penis in my face."

"Touche."

"Ready," I say as Wes palms his car keys.

"Let's roll."

The ride to the station is a silent one. Wes and I are both lost in our own thoughts. There is a connection somewhere and I'm missing it. I just know it. What Wes said this morning in the closet has been playing in my head over and over again.

Could I have spurned a lover in my past?

I thought I had left a trail of me happy with an orgasm and no strings but . . . what if I was wrong?

Wes pulls into the backlot of the police station where I work. He parks his car but doesn't shut off the engine.

"I have to go into my office for a little bit and settle some stuff," he says turning to face me.

"Okay," I say. "I'll meet up with you later. I think I want to go walk some of the crime scenes and see if anything clicks."

"Take Jones with you," he orders.

"You do know that I am a very capable police detective, right?" I roll my eyes. "I mean I know I have one of those pesky vaginas and all, but I do a pretty good job of getting the job done."

"And you know that I love you and for whatever reason, this guy is gunning for you. Is it so bad that I just want you in one piece?" he asks softly.

"No." I sigh. "I'll be careful."

"Somehow, I doubt that. But I'll let you get to it."

"Hey Wes?"

"Yeah, honey?" he answers me.

"I love you too," I tell him. "I mean I really love you."

"I really love you." He smiles that panty dropper smile at me.

"It was only ever you, Wes," I say softly as I climb out of his car and shut the door behind me. I know that it was a chicken shit move to drop an emotional bomb on him and bail—but I'm not overly comfortable with laying myself bare like that.

I push my sunglasses up on top of my head as I walk through the glass door of the station and scan the room for my man of the hour. And there he is now pouring himself a cup of coffee.

"Jones!" I shout as I head towards the kitchenette.

"What's up, Goody?" he asks me.

"I want to walk the past crime scenes today," I explain. "What do you say you come with me for a second set of eyes?"

"I have to clear it with the Captain, but if he signs off on it, sure. Sounds good to me," he smiles.

"Great!" I tell him. "Let's go talk to the dragon now."

"Maybe don't call him that to his face," Jones suggests.

"Now where is the fun in that?" I laugh.

Jones nervously follows me into Lee's office.

"And what can I do for you two this morning?" he asks Jones and I.

"I would like to go walk the crime scenes again and I want to take Jones with me for a second set of eyes," I explain.

"But I'm just finishing up here. I'm back on patrol tonight," Jones adds.

"Consider it done. I'll call Marcusen in," Lee says. "He's been asking for extra hours."

"Thank you," Jones says to Lee.

"Anytime," Lee says. "And guys?"

"Yeah," I answer.

"Yes, Sir," Jones says standing up.

"Watch your sixes. I don't like what's going on here."

"Yes, Sir," Jones repeats. I just nod before following him out of Lee's office.

"Your wheels or mine?" I ask.

"Mine," he laughs. "Yours are terrible."

I sigh. He's not wrong.

I follow Jones back out into the back lot of the police station and into the passenger seat of his cruiser. It's been awhile since I was in a patrol car. It brings back fond memories.

"Do you miss it?" he asks me.

"Sometimes," I answer. "But not the drunks. God they always puke in the backseat."

"Always," he laughs.

"I heard you're sitting the Detective's Exam next month," I say softly.

"Yeah," he answers me.

"You got this."

"You think?" he asks looking up at me nervously.

"I think you'll make a great detective, Jones," I tell him honestly.

"Thanks, Goody."

Jones pulls up at the scene of the downtown shooting and parks his cruiser. We climb out and begin walking what we know happened.

"I was here," he says pointing to where he was arguing with the drunk businessmen.

"I was over here with the young mother and her baby," I tell him.

"There were bodies here, here, and here," Jones blocks out in the street.

"And Rodriguez was with the school group over here . . ." I point out.

"So," Jones begins. "If I was the shooter, where would I be?"

That bitch.

I knew, I just knew that she would be back. In fact, I was counting on it. She thinks she can outsmart me, but she can't and I'm here to prove it to her.

She thinks she can walk away from me like that. Like I mean nothing. I am fucking everything! And I will be her everything, she just doesn't know it yet. It's frustrating to know that she should have been mine for over a year. A year, I waited for her to realize the mis-

take she made, but nothing.

Unacceptable.

And she thinks that she can flaunt someone else's ring in my face? On television no less? Absolutely not.

Oh no, my queen. It's time to pay for your sins. It's time to come home to me.

I watch her move through the scope of my rifle. Her long black waves flowing down her back and her violet eyes bright. She's so beautiful. Her curves hidden under a baggy sweatshirt and jeans. A body that I am intimately acquainted with.

I could shoot her right now and be done with it . . . but that's too quick. I have earned this reparation. She needs to atone for her year of transgressions and I am going to watch her squirm while she pays. Only then will I finally take what has been mine all along.

No, I won't kill her now . . . but soon, my queen. Soon . . .

I turn ever so slightly, and let my finger fall from the trigger guard and squeeze just enough. The report echoes along with her scream—a sound that makes my heart beat and my cock hard. It takes a powerful man to control a rifle like this and not let it control the man. That is why I am such a skilled hunter.

Now it's time to let my prey dangle for a bit . . .

"So, if I was the shooter, where would I be?" Jones asks softly as he scans the surrounding rooftops.

"I don't know," I tell him. "Now would definitely be a good time to have one of those SEALs around though."

"That's true," Jones laughs before stopping the noise abruptly. "Did you see that?"

"See what?" I ask. His words have me instantly alert.

"Maybe nothing," Jones says. "But I thought . . ." he trails off.

"You thought what?" I ask just as he shouts to me.

"Get down!" and he shoves me to the ground.

The rifle report cracks through the air. I open my eyes in time to see Jones take a hit to his shoulder and throw him backwards.

"No!" I scream. "No, no, no, no, no. Jones."

I crawl over to him and place my fingertips to his throat. He has a pulse. It's thready, but it's there. Thank God! "You stay with me, Jones. Do you hear me?" I order.

I pull my phone out of my pocket and dial the emergency line.

"9-1-1 dispatch," she answers.

"This is Detective Goodnite and I need an ambulance downtown in front of the museum," I yell. My voice is frantic.

"Tell me what's happening, Detective," she says. "I have an ambulance in route."

"Officer Jones was shot from a rooftop," I answer her.

"Can you see the shooter?"

"No," I answer.

"Are you in pursuit of the shooter?" she asks me.

"No," I answer again. "I'm with Officer Jones."

"I'm dispatching a unit as well," she tells me.

"Thank you."

"Do you have cover?" she asks me what had been bouncing around in my head from the moment Jones had told me to get down.

"No, we're sitting ducks."

I hear the sirens in the distance and send up a silent prayer of thanks. A touch to Jones's neck tells me he's hanging in there, but barely. He's still unconscious.

"You hear that, Jonesy?" I ask him softly. "Here comes the cavalry."

The paramedics come running in with a gurney and as soon as they have him stabilized and strapped to the board, they are off and running—not wasting any time that could be critical to Jones's survival.

I take off after them, refusing to leave Jones alone. After all, this is all my fault.

"Wait," I shout as I jump onto the ambulance behind Jones and the medic. "I'm coming too."

The ride to the hospital is nothing but the sporadic squawks of the driver's radio in the silent ambulance. I am used to that kind of background noise and can usually tune out what I know isn't important. But today is anything but a usual scenario.

"Here you go, ma'am," the paramedic in the back says to me. I don't even realize that I'm crying until he handed me a tissue.

"Thank you," I say as I grab the tissue from his outstretched hand.

"He's made it this far and he has a pulse," he says to me. "That's better than most GSW's we see."

"I know," I say nodding my head.

When the ambulance pulls into the hospital the quiet of the ride over is replaced by loud noises and chaos as they pull Jones off the ambulance and whisk him through the hospital doors. I'm hot on their heels until he hits the magic steel doors of the Operating Room and the nurse turns to me to tell me I am no longer allowed to follow, stopping me dead in my tracks.

"You're going to have to wait over there," she says as she points to some terrible chairs in a small room. "Someone will come for you when we know more."

I do as I'm told and go and sit in the uncomfortable chairs for who knows how long. I wait, and I wait, and I wait. I change my position. I cross my legs and uncross them, I lean forward bracing on my knees and then I lean back with my legs outstretched in front of me.

Then I get up and walk to the other side of the room where there is a coffee vending machine and fish a bunch of quarters out of my pockets. I know that the coffee is probably terrible and yet I don't care I need something to hold in my hands to keep them busy. I need to put something hot in my body to maybe warm me—just a little—from the inside out because I am overwhelmingly cold on a typical hot Indian Summer day.

I'm not just cold, I'm frozen from the inside out. I'm numb.

The machine finally stops wheezing and spits out my coffee. I slide the little door back and pick up the paper cup letting out a little yelp as I do because holy shit it's fucking hot and some just splashed on my hand

and it burns.

I walk the length of the room while I alternate blowing on my coffee and sipping it. I turn on my heels and pace the length of the room while drinking my coffee. Then I do it again and again until my coffee is gone.

I walk the length of the room one more time and toss my cup into the trashcan like Lebron freaking James but my luck is holding out today—meaning I have no luck at all—and it hits the edge of the trash can before changing its trajectory and falling to the ground.

"Shit," I bark out as I walk over and scoop up my cup this time tossing it gently into the trash can.

"Hey," a vaguely familiar man's voice sounds from behind me and I turn around. "Hey, it is you."

Shit! I know him but where do I know him from?

"Hey," I say lamely while I search for his name. Oh my God, why can't I remember where I know this guy from.

"I never saw you back at the bar after that night," he says and it all slams back. Funny how for years I have been trying to remember three days of my life that are lost to the ether but here I am remembering with an unfair clarity the night I slept with this guy to get back at Wes when he crashed into my life almost a year ago and demanded his place there.

Fuck me running I cannot catch a break today.

"Matt?" I ask. "No, Mike, it's Mike, right?"

"Mark, actually." And I swear it was there for a split second but an anger like I have never seen before flashes across his face. Mark is pissed, no, Mark loathes me? His intense dislike for me or this situation is gone before I can ever really put a name to it.

"I'm so sorry," I explain. "It's been a really bad week but that doesn't excuse my rudeness."

"It's fine," he says.

"It's not but thank you for being gracious. So how have you been?" I ask.

"Good, I'm getting married soon," he tells me and that makes my smile which was forced to start spread wide across my face.

"That's awesome," I congratulate him. "Me too."

"What a coincidence," he says looking over his shoulder. "Well, it was nice seeing you, but I better get going."

"Sure, have a good night."

After he walks out the hospital doors, I sit down and place my face in my hands. God my life was such a mess a year ago. I can't believe that I used and discarded that nice guy and so many more just like him while I was in such a bad place. I can't help feeling like a total asshole.

"Claire," I hear my name and look up. Wes is rushing through the glass doors.

"Wes," I run and jump into his arms. Oh, how I need him right now.

"I got here as soon as I could," he tells me.

"It's okay, you're here now and that's all that matters."

"What's going on?" he asks me. "Any word."

"No word," I tell him. "I don't even know what time it is."

"It's about seven o'clock."

"Shit," I say.

"Baby, what happened?" he asks me.

I take a deep breath and roll my shoulders back to shore up my courage before explaining. "Jones and I went to the downtown site to block out what happened and bounce ideas off of each other."

"Yeah, we talked about that this morning."

"H-h-he was there," I barely get the words out.

"Who was there?" Wes asks me.

"The Hunter," I answer.

"Fuck!" Wes bites out.

"I know," I say as the tears I thought I had under control begin rolling down my cheeks again. "He was on top of one of the buildings just waiting for us. I think Jones saw him because he yelled at me to get down. H-h-he saved me, Wes."

"He's a good man and a good cop, Claire," Wes explains.

In my mind I know that Wes is right. Jones is a great man and an even better cop. If he gets the chance to sit the Detective's Exam I know that he'll blow it out of the water, but that's a big if right now. I think the part that sticks with me the most is that none of this would be happening right now if he wasn't with me today. He would be fine and healthy and having dinner with his wife, Linda right now if he wasn't my friend.

Because at the end of the day, we all know that this is my fault. Sure, not directly, but somehow, some way, I was the catalyst for a madman to become a mass murderer.

Wes sits with me for I don't know how long, just holding me and gently rubbing my back. What he doesn't do is promise me that everything will be all okay in the morning, because that's a promise we both know he couldn't keep. I'm not sure anything will be okay in the morning.

"I need to go wrap up a few more things before I head home. Do you want me to come get you after?" he asks me.

"No, I think I need to be here," I tell him.

"Okay," Wes says softly. "Do you want me to come back and stay here with you?" Wes asks me.

"No, it's okay," I answer him. "There's no reason for both of us to be miserable."

"But I'm miserable without you," he says as he tucks my hair behind my ear.

"Then, yeah, come back for me." I smile at him.

"I will," Wes promises me. "I'll always come back for you."

He kisses me on the forehead and walks out the door. Too bad I would find out later, I should have asked Wes to stay with me and not go back to the office because I would find out later that it would be the difference between life and death.

Sometime after Wes leaves, Lee walks in with Linda and I immediately jump to my feet when I see them. Linda's face is red and splotchy with tears stains down her cheeks. She looks terrible as she leans on Lee for support. It's then that it dawns on me, that if something like this ever happened to Wes, I wouldn't survive it. I know that now.

"Come sit down," I say as I help usher Linda to the seat next to the one I was sitting in.

"Thanks," she says.

"Can I get you a coffee or anything?" I ask.

"No, I'm okay," she says. "Has there been any

word?"

"No," I answer as I shake my head. Linda's face crumples as she sobs into the wad of tattered tissue she has clenched in her fist.

"Linda," I start. I have to swallow past the lump in my throat a couple of times before I can say what I need to say. "I am so sorry. This is all my fault."

"No!" she shouts. I deserve her anger and now we both know it.

"Yes, this killer is punishing me for something, I don't know what, but it's my fault Jones was hit," I explain.

"No!" she snaps again taking my hand and sandwiching it tight between her two. "Don't you dare take responsibility for that monster. My husband would be furious if he could hear you right now. You're no more responsible for his being shot than I am, and I don't want to hear you suggest otherwise."

"Okay," I say softly for lack of anything better to say.

"Good," she says firmly. "It's done now."

"Mrs. Jones," the Dr. in the doorway calls out.

"That's me," Linda says as she jumps to her feet. "I-i-is my husband alright?"

"He's out of surgery and stable but he's not out of the woods yet," the surgeon tells her.

"Is he awake? Can I see him?" she asks the hope in her voice ringing out for all to hear.

"You may go and see him now but know that your husband is in a coma." Her face falls again.

"Is he going to wake up?" she asks.

"My hope is that he will when his body has healed

some. Right now, he needs rest so that's what his body is doing," he tells her.

"Okay. We can do that," she says as she rolls her shoulders back. "Now take me to my husband please."

Linda looks back to where Lee and I are standing. My brother seems to read her mind when he tells her, "We'll be right here, Linda. Don't worry, we're here for you."

"Thanks, Captain, Claire," she says before following the surgeon through the big metal doors.

It's time. It's finally time to take what is mine, but first I have to make her pay. She thinks she can be with that FBI agent on the news. That he is better than me, well I will show her.

What better way to make my queen come to me then to remove her king from the board? When she realizes what I have done I bet she comes running. Then I will show her who the real king is once and for all.

Oh, here he comes now . . .

"Excuse me!" I shout to get his attention. He looks tired and frustrated. Good. Now it's time to play . . .

chapter 18

well, fuck.

Wes

THIS CASE IS DRIVING me fucking nuts.

It's always a fun fucking day when you realize that you are hunting a freaking psycho who has decided he has an unhealthy fixation on your woman. Also, it's never a good freaking day when you realize that this exact scenario has happened more than once. This year.

I swear on all that's holy that when we solve this fucking nightmare of a case and Claire and I finally—fucking finally—get married I am going to take her on the vacation to end all vacations and make us both transfer to outstanding parking tickets because this is ridiculous.

And speaking of nightmares . . . it is killing me slowly to wake up to another one of her devastation half memories every night. I pray to God every night that she either remembers or forgets once and for all. But I will tough it out and keep my trap shut because whatever those nightmares may do to me is nothing in comparison to the hell that my girl has been living in for twenty-four fucking years.

I let out a heavy sigh and run my hands through my hair as I push through the automatic glass doors of the hospital. My frustration is boiling too close to the surface and I hate that. I prefer to stay cool, calm, and collected.

"Excuse me," I hear someone call out. I look over my shoulder and see a man that looks vaguely familiar.

"Can I help you?" I ask the man.

"Oh my God, thank you," he says. "I didn't know who else to ask but my car won't start. Can you take a look at it for me?"

I want to tell this guy no because it's been a long fucking day and I have a metric shit ton of stuff to do before I can get back here to be with Claire while we wait for news on Jones. But that's not why I do what I do, and this guy is in the hospital parking lot, so he was obviously visiting someone too—so his day is probably just as shitty as mine. So, I turn to him and do what I always knew I would do. Too bad it will turn out to be a big fucking mistake.

"Sure man," I tell him. "Pop the hood."

I hear the click of the latch on the hood of a Suburban that looks brand fucking new and wonder why it's having problems but I don't really know now do I?

I raise the hood and prop it with the post to hold it open and lean down to take a look.

"I don't really see anything out of the ordinary," I tell him. "Why don't you try and start it, so I can hear what it sounds like?"

But he doesn't do that.

Instead, I feel something hard and heavy hit the back of my head and my knees give out. I crumple to the floor as my vision waivers and it's like watching the tuner going out on an old television.

"Thanks ever so much for your assistance," the man says as he smiles down at me. "Please allow me to introduce myself. I'm The Hunter."

And then everything goes black . . .

Well, fuck.

chapter 19

not okay

Claire

"**H**E'S GOING TO BE okay, right?" I ask.

"I don't know," Lee tells me, and I let out a heavy sigh. I just feel so defeated.

"You okay, kid?" Lee asks me when we sit back down.

"Not really," I admit.

"You don't say," he drolls and I roll my eyes.

"You know you're kind of a mess yourself," I tell him something I'm sure he already knows.

"This isn't about me, kid," Lee says trying to change the subject again. "This is about you."

"I know," I answer him and also don't. "And also, it's really not. Tonight is about Jones."

"Yeah," my brother says.

"He told me today that he was going to sit the De-tective's Exam," I tell Lee.

"He is," my brother confirms. "He's going to make a damn fine detective."

"Better than me," I say trying to lighten the mood.

"Everyone is a better detective than you," Lee laughs.

"Thanks, asshole."

"I'll be here all night."

"While, we're playing group therapy session," I wade in.

"Claire—" he starts to cut me off, but I don't let him finish.

"For real, Lee," I push back. "Right now, it's just you and me so tell me the truth. What's going on with you and Emma?"

"I still love her," he says.

"Well, that sounds promising."

"And she still blames me for Anna's death and hates my guts."

"That doesn't sound so good," I tell him.

"But every night she shows up at my house to ride my dick and then leave us both feeling empty in a room full of self-loathing."

"Wow, I'm sorry I asked," I tell him.

"Yeah, it's not great." He shrugs.

"What are you going to do?" I ask him.

"What can I do?"

"I don't know," I admit.

"I need her so much that I will take whatever she gives me and be happy. It's less than I deserve so I'll take it. If she can't ever love me back or forgive me, then that's okay. If all she wants is my cock, then that's fine too."

"It's not fine," I sigh.

"No, it's not, but it's what I have."

"Also, don't ever say 'cock' in front of me again."

"You brought that on yourself," he says on a smug smile.

"Did I ever tell you about the time Wes tied me up and spanked me?"

"Stop!" Lee shouts. "You win! I quit!"

I laugh. "Never mess with the master!"

"Let's just try and get a little shut eye, alright?" Lee suggests.

"Sure," I say as I tip my head back against the wall and try not to imagine all the hospital germs crawling around all over this room and close my eyes. Before I know it, it works and I'm asleep.

Run!

I'm running as fast as my little feet will take me through the woods behind my parents' house. I have to get away from the bad man. If he catches me now, I'll never get away. I have to be free.

Run! I have to run faster.

I see the blue gray light as it spills through the trees. Mommy always told me this was her favorite part of the day—Looking at the sun as it comes up in the morning. I ran away late in the night when the bad man came for me one more time. It was my only chance. After I found the baseball bat in the pile of old junk at the back of the closet I knew what I had to do. I'm so glad I made Wes and Lee teach me how to play ball with them because now I'm free.

Free.

I'm free. Those are the words in my head as the tree break and I see Wes standing at the edge of the backyard. I'm free. I'm finally free. Wes looks up and he sees me.

"I've got her!" he shouts to someone.

My heart is beating so hard in my chest and it hurts to breathe. I'm so tired but I have to keep running. I see Wes, his face, I know that he'll protect me. Wes always protects me. He will keep me safe. He will keep me free.

I push my feet just a little harder, I run just a little faster. I'm almost there. I'm almost free when a strong hand wraps around my arm so hard that it hurts, pulling me around to face him, not Wes, the bad man. Wes is gone and the only person near me is the man I would do anything to get away from.

"No!" I scream.

"You're mine, Claire. You'll never be free."

"Jesus Christ!" Lee shouts as I bolt upright in my seat. "What the fuck was that?"

"Nothing, Lee," I tell him. "Just go back to sleep."

"I can't go back to sleep," he practically shouts. "You were fucking screaming."

"I wasn't screaming," I deny. In all truth, I was probably screaming but my brother doesn't need to know that.

"Yes, you were," he tells me. "Is it always like this?"

I let out a sigh before admitting, "Mostly."

"Jesus," he mutters. "You need to get help, Claire."

"Thanks, asshole," I growl. "I was but my therapist died so excuse me if I don't want to run out and get another one."

"Claire—" he starts but I won't let him finish.

"Just let it go."

"Does Wes know about this?" he asks me on a low voice.

"Of course Wes knows," I tell him. "He's with me every night."

A frown pulls at my brow and I look at the time on the lock screen of my phone. It's after three in the morning and Wes isn't back yet. He said he was coming back.

"What's wrong?" Lee asks, accurately assessing the change in my mood.

"It's after three in the morning and Wes isn't here," I explain.

"I don't understand," Lee says.

"Before you guys got here, Wes was leaving," I explain. "He said that he had some more stuff to wrap up at the office and then he was going to grab a change of clothes before coming back here to be with me."

"But he's not here now," Lee states the obvious that has acid burning in my stomach.

"No, he's not."

"Try calling him," Lee suggests.

I pick up my phone and dial Wes's phone number.

It rings several times before going to voicemail, "Hi. You've reached Wes, leave me a message at the beep."

"Well?" he asks.

"Voicemail."

"Let me try," he says. I watch my brother pull his phone out of his pocket and dial his best friend before frowning at his phone and then hitting the button to end the call.

"Well?" I ask.

"It rang three times and then went to voicemail," he tells me.

"Shit!" I bite out.

"Wes always answers his phone."

"Let me try him again," I say but I don't get the chance because my phone dings with a text message from Wes's phone.

> WES: this is the hunter meet me at this address or you'll never see your beau again.

"I think I know where Wes is," I whisper.

"Where?" Lee asks.

I hold up my phone to show him the text. "I think he's with The Hunter."

"God damnit!"

I furiously text him back asking the question I know that I don't want the answer to but for Wes, I have to. I love Wes that much. I would do anything for him.

> ME: What do you want?

> WES: You. It's time to pay for your crimes.

"What are you doing?" Lee asks when I grab my

phone and jump out of my seat.

"I have to go get him."

"Not on your fucking own, Claire," he shouts. "That's suicide. Let me get a team together."

"I can't wait, Lee," I tell him. "You get a team together, I have to leave now."

"No," he says standing there between me and the door, unmoving. Like a stone in the middle of a riverbed. I'll just have to go around him, and I know exactly how to do it.

"What if it was Emma?" I ask quietly.

"That's not fair," he says.

"I'll never play fair where Wes is concerned, brother of mine," I tell him gently. "I love him so much that I know that I would not survive this world without him."

"We're right behind you," he sighs. "This is going against everything that I know is right."

"I know, me too."

"Then don't do it," Lee pleads.

"I have to."

"Claire—"

"If I don't make it," I start.

"Don't talk like that," he orders.

"If I don't make it," I tell him. "Name your first kid after me!"

"What if it's a boy?" he shouts as I'm running out the door.

"Then that sucks for him!" I shout as I race to my car.

Shit! I don't have a car. I see a cab stopped at the curb just down the way and I take off running for it. "Taxi! Taxi!" I shout as my phone pings one more time with a pin drop to my maps. Got to love advancing technology when the bad guy can tell you where to find him with a text message.

chapter 20

showtime

*S*tupid bitch!

I am so disappointed in her. She thinks she can come here and save her precious boyfriend. As if I would ever let her! She needs to learn some manners and I am just the man to teach them to her.

She is not the winner of this game. She can't be because I am the game maker! I make the rules and I am the true victor here.

I pull the ropes just a little tighter around the big idiot in the chair. This bar has been closed for a while now. I bought the building and wouldn't let them renew their lease because I have been waiting for almost a year just for this moment.

She chose me over him that night and now it's time to remind her why I am the superior candidate. Not him.

I bet she's almost here. Showtime!

chapter 21

what took you so long?

"**W**HAT THE HELL?"

This can't be it. The taxi pulls over at the old bar I used to frequent from time to time when I was looking for guys to hook-up with in a no strings attached kind of a situation.

But this place is boarded up and run down.

In the year that Wes and I have tap danced around each other to finally get our shit together and be an us, this place has gone to shit. I let my mind wander back to the last time that I was here . . .

"The usual?" Joe, my favorite bartender asks as I walk in.

"Yeah," I smile and take a seat at the end of the bar where I can watch the people who move around the establishment and pick my next victim.

Joe slides the seven and seven on a cocktail napkin in front of me. I smile my thanks as I pick up my drink and take a sip. I swivel around on my barstool and watch the crowd absentmindedly. There's a couple of cute guys, but nobody peaks my interest.

I feel someone sit down next to me and I look up. He's about five-eleven or six foot with a mop a sandy blonde hair and brown eyes. He has an easy smile and he immediately turns it my way. I look back at Joe who winks and shakes his head. He knows my drill.

He looks at me and smiles, "I'll have what she's having," he says to Joe and I think he might do. But I'm just not that into it. I'll see how it goes.

Joe slides the drink in front of him and he happily sips his drink while waiting for me to say something. I finally decide to help him out.

"Well, what do you think?" I ask.

"I think it's not bad. Is it your signature drink?"

"I don't have a signature . . ." But I'm stopped by Joe.

"She does, and it is."

"I'm Mark," he smiles at me and holds out his hand for me to shake. As I take his hand in mine and notice a firm grip on a smooth hand with no calluses and clean trimmed fingernails. The callous on my index finger grazes his knuckles and he bites his lip.

"I'm Claire," I say smiling.

"So Claire, do you live around here?" he asks. "Wow, was that as bad as it sounded?" I laugh.

I feel eyes on me and I start to scan the room but come up short when I see Wes scowling from a table in the corner. A waitress with a trim waist and balloons for boobs grazes his elbow with her rock-hard nipple as she delivers his drink, a cold beer in the bottle, but his gaze stays locked on me. I roll my eyes and turn back to Mark.

"No, it wasn't that bad," I lie.

"So what do you do, Claire?" Mark asks.

Joe groans.

I bite my lip and shake my head no. I'm not going to tell him. It will end all the fun. There's no way Mr. Businessman or Mr. Lawyer wants to go home with a police detective. I look over at his polo shirt and jeans and think he's cute in a very country club sort of way.

"Oh, you want me to guess do you?"

I smile wider because he'll never guess and nod my head. I sip my drink and wait for him to guess. This could be fun. And I need fun. The missing boy, Anthony, and Wes and our fucked up past have my emotions too close to the surface.

"A dental hygienist."

"Ew, gross. I would never stick my hands in people's mouths." I laugh. Although I have stuck them in a dead body so what does that say about me?

"A librarian."

"Do I look like a librarian to you?" I laugh.

"Only in my dreams," he laughs. "That was cheesy too, right?"

"Yeah, kind of. What about you? What do you do?" I ask. I feel eyes on me again and I look over my shoulder. The waitress with the flotation devices and the huge hair is sitting in his lap, his ear is caught between her teeth. They're crooked, I notice uncharitably. I'll drop an extra twenty in the offerings tray on Sunday

and ask for forgiveness. It was worth it.

"You know that guy?" Mark asks.

I look back at him and see him looking at Wes and the hooker. "No," I say as I look at him. He's handsome and nice. I should choose a guy like him. I toss the remainder of my drink back and ask, "You want to get out of here?"

"Hell, yes."

"Your place, I'll follow you out," I tell him as I stand. Mark throws some money on the bar top for Joe and I see him tip his imaginary hat at me behind Mark's back as thanks for the huge tip. Or maybe it's my ability to leave with a guy in less than an hour. I mentally shrug, who knows.

As I found out following his nondescript sedan home, Mark lives around the corner from my local bar. That's going to be awkward later. I pull into the visitor spot closest to where he parked his car. He waits for me by the door like a gentleman and then leads me up the stairs to his second-floor apartment.

Mark holds the door open for me but as soon as it closes behind me I grab him by the shirt and pull him against my body, breast to chest, and kiss him deeply. Not bad. Not great, but not bad. Mr. Country Club is not an aggressive lover.

He breaks away from my body to push my jacket over my shoulders. I pull his polo over his head and toss it to the ground. Mark sees to it that my t-shirt and bra go the same way. He smiles his coy smile at me again before taking my hand and leading me to his bedroom where I make my second major mistake of the night.

And it snaps back into place like a rubber band.

I know exactly who has Wes. My skin crawls at the idea that so many people had died because of someone I hooked up with the better part of a year ago. I think of Rodriguez, Matt, and Jasmine cut down in their prime and then I think of Jones fighting for his life in a hospital bed.

How stupid I was. I bet he laughed when he left there. He saw me in the waiting room and pretended to give a shit but really, he was there to bask in how low he brought me.

That son of a bitch!

"Thanks, man," I say as I hand the cab driver a bunch of bills. And watch him peel out from the curb like his pants were on fire.

I don't even blame him. This neighborhood doesn't look so good anymore.

I don't have anything left to lose but Wes and I'm not willing to wait for the cavalry to get here before going in. I need to know that Wes is alright, that he's even still alive. Although, I feel like in my soul I would know if he wasn't. That on a cellular level, we are connected enough that if something really happened to Wes, I would know. As hokey as it sounds, it's true.

I push open the door to the bar and step inside. When I do, I see the reason for the smug smile on his sadistic fucking face, and there he sits, happy as you please, with Wes in the chair on the other side of the table and a gun pointed directly at the love of my life. Wes, the one man I could ever love is tied to a fucking chair with a gun pointed at his head.

"Hello, Claire," he greets me.

"Hello, Mark."

"I'm so glad you could join me tonight," he says like he has invited me out to the opera or a fancy dinner party. So not creepy at all . . .

"And where exactly am I?" I ask him. I want him to tell me what's going on even though I'm pretty sure I can read between the lines, even here in crazy town.

"We're where it all began," he says as he waves his gun arm around. "I bought this place for you."

"Charming, I love what you've done with the place," I snark.

"Don't be cruel," he snaps. "You are the one that made me play all of these silly games."

"Silly games?" I question as shock rolls over my body one inch at a time. "You call killing tons of innocent people and good cops silly games?"

"Of course," he waves his gun hand again. Those people don't mean anything to me."

"You're crazy," I whisper. "Abso-fucking-lutely stark raving mad, bat shit crazy. Bonkers."

"Don't be rude!" he snaps. "It's time now."

"Time for what?" I ask suddenly feeling nervous. I need to stall. I need everyone else to get here and save the day now that I know that Wes is alive.

"This is it, Claire," he tells me.

"What is it?" I ask again. I'm still standing in the entryway to the old bar.

"This is when you lose," he says cryptically. "Why don't you come in and take your coat off."

"Did you think I would let you have him? Did you think that I didn't see you look at each other all night?" he demands, and I have no idea who he is or what he's talking about.

"What?"

"You're mine, Claire! And now you have to pay. You thought I'd let you leave me for him, that you could use me as a pawn in your slut games, but I am the ultimate hunter."

And then it all snaps into place. I thought he was a random, someone I could use and forget way back when I was avoiding Wes and all commitments. I left this guy in his apartment one night and never looked back. How could I have been so stupid? And the worst part is, I never even remembered his name until I saw him again at the hospital last night while I was waiting on word on Jones.

"I grew up hunting in the woods with my grandfather. He was one mean bastard too. He believed in being accurate with the first shot, not the second so a bunch of stupid cops were nothing to me. But like I said before, you had to pay."

"Stupid," I snap. "Jasmine was not stupid. She was good, and she was kind but she was not stupid. She was on her dinner break eating a fucking hamburger you monster!"

"Soon you'll be screaming my name, Claire, but I'm okay if you like to call out monster too. I just want to hear you scream."

"In your dreams, pal."

"No, Claire, in yours. How's that going by the way?" He's too young to be my kidnapper so I know that he's baiting me but still the idea that he knows my inner thoughts and terrors rankles.

"Just peachy," I snark.

"You think you're so smart. So tough and strong. Brave even. I wonder what you'll be like when I really hit you where it hurts. How will you feel when you watch pretty boy here die at my hands?"

"I'll be just fine because you aren't going to hurt him," I say bold as you please while inside I am shaking in my converse sneakers.

"Say goodbye, Claire," he says as he pulls back the hammer, but he never gets the chance. I pull my side arm from the back of my pants just the way Wes and I joked about earlier that morning and fire center mass just like I was taught.

"Goodbye, asshole." And then I empty the rest of my magazine into the center of his chest for good measure.

"What took you so long?" Wes demands.

"I'm sorry." I wink at Wes. "It's been a long night."

"Well, try not to let it happen again," he says with laughter in his voice. "Seriously, it's good to see you. That dude was bananas."

"I kind of got that impression."

"Funny," he rolls his eyes.

"I'm not gonna lie, I'm kind of enjoying being the one to do the saving this time," I tell him as I start to untie the ropes around him. "You can be the hero next time though. I wouldn't want to wound your precious male pride."

"This time?!" Wes yells and then winces like his head is killing him. "There isn't going to be a next time, Claire."

"Sure, baby. Whatever you say."

chapter 22

rehearsal

One week later . . .

I FUSS WITH THE white eyelet sundress that I have just slipped over my head in front of a large oval mirror in my suite at the shore.

Three hours ago, Emma pulled up to the house in a convertible she had rented for the weekend.

"What's all this?" I had asked her.

"We need to live a little," she had explained. "It's been a rough couple of months."

"No kidding."

So, we had loaded up my dress and my suitcase into the backseat and headed down the coast singing to the radio with our hair blowing in the wind. It was the best time I had had in a long time. The stress of this case and the guilt that I carry has been riding me hard lately. While Jones pulled out of his coma a few days ago, he's still holed up at the hospital while they make sure he has everything he needs for a full recovery with his wife, Linda, at his side. And I'm sure next month he's going to kick the Detective's Exam's ass.

Emma had pulled into the circle in front of the resort and let the bellhop unload our bags with a quick, "Be careful with that one," she had said point to my dress bag. "It's precious cargo." and a fifty-dollar bill for his trouble.

"You just made that kid's day," I had told her.

"Shh," Emma had stage whispered. "I don't want people to think I have a heart."

"I think you have the biggest heart of all."

We check into the hotel and settle into the honeymoon suite where Emma and I will spend tonight and get dressed for the wedding tomorrow. Then Wes and I will spend our wedding night here.

"So, this is where the magic is going to happen," Emma had joked as she flopped down on her back on the big, fluffy bed with all of its down pillows and duvet.

"But of course," I had laughed. She had swatted me with a pillow until we both laughed until we cried.

"I guess we should get ready for this big dinner that Wes's stuffy parents are holding in your honor tonight," she had said without even trying to pretend to be excited.

"Be nice," I had warned her.

"Yeah, yeah, yeah."

I had brushed out my windswept hair into thick, beachy waves and applied a little makeup to my face. I want to be pretty, but I don't want to look like I'm trying too hard. Tomorrow, though, I'm going to knock Wes's socks off with my wedding day glitz and glam.

I took my dress, on its hanger, into the bathroom

and changed into it, slipping the delicate material over my head and pulling up the side zipper.

When I stepped out of the bathroom I am greeted by the sight of Emma in a soft pink sundress and sandals looking absolutely beautiful and surprisingly sweet and delicate.

"More pink?" I had asked her.

"It felt right at the time," she had said nervously. "But now I'm not so sure."

"You look beautiful," I had told her before turning to the mirror to fuss at my dress.

I, too, don't feel overly comfortable in girly clothing. What a pair Emma and I must be.

Now, we stand here side by side looking bewildered and frightened which is ridiculous considering we're both kind of badass bitches.

I trace a finger over the scar on my shoulder. It's a reminder that I will have for the rest of my life that some mistakes stay with you for eternity and have very lasting consequences. Jasmine is one of those consequences. So is Jones, but he's getting there. He also told me yesterday that if I apologize one more time he's going to kick my ass when he gets back to work.

I told him he's on and that I can't wait.

I trace the silvery line on my shoulder one more time before Emma sighs and swats my hand away.

"Stop that!"

"I can't help it," I admit.

"I have it on good authority, that men dig scars, so let it go," she tells me.

"I know," I sigh. "I just feel so . . . guilty."

"Well, you have to stop that," she admonishes.

"Hello pot, paging kettle," I laugh. Emma is one to talk about guilt the way she's hanging on to hers after Anna's death.

"I know." She sighs. "Let's just try and enjoy this weekend and get you hitched, okay?"

"I'll make a deal with you," I offer up.

"I'm not sure I want to know."

"I'll relax and enjoy the weekend if you do too."

She lets out another heavy sigh. I'm clearly trying her patience this weekend. "Okay, fine. I'll relax and enjoy the weekend too."

"Good. Now let's go and get this rehearsal show on the road before we're late for dinner."

Emma and I walked down to the wedding venue arm in arm like the opening scene of Laverne and Shirley. Just two independent women, ready to take on the world, or in this case, a wedding weekend for the society pages.

"There you are!" the wedding planner shouts just a little too loud. It makes me wonder if she thought I wouldn't show or something.

Wes walks up to me and kisses me sweetly on the lips. "You look beautiful."

"Thanks," I say suddenly feeling shy.

"Glad you could make it," he smiles at me and I can't help but to smile back.

"Were you afraid I wouldn't come?" I ask.

His eyes heat and he leans down to whisper in my ear, "Oh, I know you'll come. I just wasn't one hundred percent sure you would turn up for this dog and pony show."

"Thanks for the glowing vote of confidence," I

snark. "Maybe I changed my mind."

I start to pull away from Wes, but he laughs as he grabs my hand and pulls me back against him. "Not so fast."

"Ugh. Fine. I guess you're stuck with me."

"Happily," he tells me.

"Places, people!" the wedding planner calls out.

Wes and his mom are in the front of the lineup. He is supposed to walk her to her seat next to his dad and then stand at the altar and wait for me. I'm hoping she doesn't start slinging her shit this weekend but really, we all know it's just a matter of time. While she's my mom's best friend, she has never thought that I was good enough for her son. It's been getting worse the closer Wes and I grew to each other.

My late sister, Bonnie's children line up next to each other with Lee and Emma behind them. I feel bad for making them walk down the aisle together, but Emma is my Maid of Honor and Lee is Wes's Best Man. They don't have a choice. Also, I'm secretly hoping forcing them together for the weekend will make them finally work their shit out once and for all because they clearly are miserable without each other and if anything, the last year has taught us that life is infinitely too short.

My parents and I are in the back. I have chosen to have both my parents walk me down the aisle and honor my mom. It's a break from tradition but she's been the best mom I could have asked for and this moment is all about celebrating our family, so it just felt right.

"Okay, here's what we're going to do," the wedding planner instructs everyone to their places and I love watching her order everyone around. It's kind of fun.

Wes winks at me from his place at the altar and I have this overwhelming sense that this is it. This is where I am meant to be. The road here was not an easy one, but life with Wes will be totally worth it. To be loved by this man, so wholly and completely is more than I deserve but I am unwilling to live without him.

My parents and I are halfway up the aisle before the wedding planner turns around and gasps in horror. Well, it looks like my run of shitty luck is holding after all . . .

"What are you doing?" she yells.

"Umm . . . rehearsing?" I ask confused.

"The bride does not walk up the aisle any other time than when she walks to her groom for real. It's bad luck. Like really, really bad luck."

"Whoops." I shrug.

I see Wes behind her laughing and shaking his head at me. He looks carefree and unconcerned so I figure we'll be alright but I can't help the feeling of doom that just hit the pit of my stomach.

After thoroughly horrifying the wedding planner with my epic run of bad luck, she walks everyone through their duties for the big day. The whole time Wes smiles at me like I am the most important person in the world.

"Alright, everyone," the wedding planner claps her hands. "That's a wrap! Go enjoy dinner and don't get drunk!"

"I'm totally getting drunk," Lee mumbles as he walks by. It will be an act of God if Emma doesn't act like she's been touched by a leper every time she has to take Lee's arm. Everyone winced when she would flinch as he reached for her.

"Me too," Emma mumbles as we head for the restaurant where our rehearsal dinner is being hosted by Wes's parents.

I kind of want to get drunk too. Those two are going to take ten years off of my life with the way they keep going on and on.

"Well," my dad breaks into my thoughts. "I have been looking forward to this day for your entire life."

"Dad," I whisper smiling at him.

"You picked a good guy," he tells me. "But then again, I never doubted you."

"I love you, Dad." I hug him tight.

"And I love you, baby. Now let's go watch Emma and Lee makes asses of themselves." I throw my head back and laugh.

"Sounds good, Dad," I tell him and let him escort me into the restaurant where everyone is waiting.

When we sit down at the tables that are pre-arranged for our party, I see that the beer and champagne is already flowing. And along with the rest of our families, the SEALs are in attendance. This should be interesting.

I look to their table, and everyone is laughing and smiling but Surfer. He has a dark longing on his face that I can't put a finger on. I bet there's a story there.

"Don't go there," Wes warns low for my ears only when he joins me at my side.

"Go where?" I ask innocently.

"Leave Surfer alone."

"He's across the room, how can I possibly bother

him?"

"Just leave him alone. If you have to meddle, meddle with Lee and Emma, but Surfer has his own demons to expunge."

"That sounds mysterious."

"Just leave it alone."

"Yes, Sir," I snap.

"Mmm, you have no idea what those words from your lips do to me, baby," Wes says as he bites his bottom lip. "Let's try that tomorrow night."

My cheeks heat at his dirty suggestion and the table of SEALs clearly don't miss it as they start hooting and hollering and making their own lewd suggestions. Wes just laughs. And Lee shakes his head covering his ears which makes me laugh too.

The dinner service is my favorite meal of beef wellington, mashed potatoes, and cooked spinach. Wes planned this dinner all by himself and he clearly thought of me when he planned the menu. It warms my heart to know that he knows me so thoroughly.

Wes clinks his dessert spoon against his wine glass as he stands up from his seat beside me at the table.

"If I could have your attention," he says as the room quiets down. "As you all know, Claire and I have had a long road to get to this moment right now and you all have been part of that, so thank you for helping us get here.

"Claire, you are by far, the greatest thing to come into my life and I would be lost without you."

"Wes," I say smiling up at him. "I love you."

"So, I got you a little something to show you what an honor it is to be chosen by you," he says as he hands me a light blue bag.

I open the bag to reveal to light blue boxes under the white tissue paper. The first one that I open, a small square box, holds two glittering diamond solitaires twinkling at me from the white satin pad and I immediately put them on. It is exactly what I would have chosen for myself.

"Thank you so much," I tell him.

"Keep going," he says on a smile.

The next blue box is long and rectangular and holds a matching diamond tennis bracelet on its satin bed. It's stunning and while I wouldn't wear it every day, I will wear it on every special occasion and think of Wes in this moment.

I hold out my wrist for him to slip it on and after he buckles the clasp, Wes kisses my pulse point under my wrist.

"Thank you," I mouth to him.

"My pleasure," he rumbles.

"Yes, I think it will be," I whisper. Wes's eyes heat and twinkle at my blatant suggestion in front of our closest friends and family.

"And lastly," he tells the room. "Long ago, I gave Claire my most prized possession when she was just a little girl. I have no idea where it went, and I bet she doesn't either, but it was way back then that she stole my heart along with my favorite baseball cap. So in honor of her finally making me the happiest man in the world, I bought her her own."

Wes pulls from behind his back a Yankees ball cap. It's brand new with tags still on it and the dark navy of the hat is stark and unmarred against the white stitching of the NY on the front. I look at him and this hat a little confused. I don't remember Wes ever giving me a hat and that makes me sad.

"I forgot about that hat," my dad says. "Whatever happened to it, Claire?"

"I have no idea," I say honestly.

"You wound me, baby." Wes laughs.

"Thank heaven," my mother says, her voice full of laughter. "She wore that thing everywhere. Backwards too with her long hair hanging down. I finally had a girl to dress in ribbons and lace and you heathens taught her to spit and pitch a ball instead."

"Man, she had an awesome swing though," Lee says, his voice ringing with pride for his little sister.

Wes places the cap on my head, backwards and tucks my hair behind my ears and it all comes rushing back.

I was six years old, and the boys had just taught me how to hit a baseball.

"Damn, she's good," Wes had said his voice ringing with pride.

"Did you think my sister would be anything but?" Lee asked.

"Well, she is your sister." Wes had laughed.

"Yeah, and she's perfect."

"She is," Wes had agreed. "So perfect, I think she's earned a prize." He pulled the worn and battered and obviously well-loved Yankees cap off of his head and placed it on mine, tucking my hair back behind my ears just as he did now.

Three weeks after that beautiful moment in my parents' backyard with my brother and his best friend, the man I would eventually marry, I was wearing that ball cap when I made my escape attempt. I must have left it behind in that closet. My stomach pitches at the thought. That something so beautiful could be tainted by something so dirty, so foul.

"Thank you, Wes," I tell him. "I love it."

"And I love you," he tells me as he places a soft kiss on my mouth.

The night moves on with more laughter and stories of Wes and I growing up. His parents do not join in the merriment.

"Will you excuse me for a moment?" I ask him. "I'm just going to run to the ladies' room for a minute."

"Sure, baby," he says with a touch of concern in his eyes. "Everything alright?"

"Yeah, I think all the wine just got to me," I lie. I'm going to be sick. My stomach pitches and somersaults all over the place.

"Just don't be too long," he says, and I watch the heat flare in his eyes one more time. How this man can love me so much after all that we have been through still amazes me more and more every day.

He kisses me again, this time a little deeper and the SEALs go wild. I roll my eyes and push away from the table. I head towards the restroom and pause halfway across the room to look over my shoulder at Wes who has his sole focus on me. If only I had paid more attention to the rest of the occupants of the room, I would have noticed that someone else paid me too much attention as well.

When I enter the ladies room I walk into the stall and drop to my knees before losing the entire contents of my stomach into the toilet. As I heave, I think of that dark closet, where I left behind Wes's most prized possession and I hate whoever took me with my entire being. Why can't I remember?

I flush the toilet and move to the sink to wash my hands. I cup water to my mouth to rinse the vomit out and grab a paper towel from the holder to try and repair the mascara that ran when I puked.

It's pretty good. I don't look great, but I'll just blame it on the wine when I get back to the table. When I push the door open, I never see him coming, I only feel a hand cover my nose and mouth. A cloying scent fills my lungs and then it's lights out . . .

chapter 23

left behind

IT'S DARK. SO DARK. *At night my mommy leaves a nightlight on for me and my favorite piggy stuffed animal that I've had for ages to help me sleep. I hate the dark. Monsters only lurk in the dark. I want my mommy, but I can't cry. If I cry, the bad man will come, and he will hurt me again. He always hurts me. Even though I don't want him to, I know, he always comes, but this time I will be ready.*

I was digging in the closet when I knew that he was asleep. I found a pile of old junk. He must have been too lazy to clean out the closet that has been my prison for I don't know how long. But his laziness is my win. In the corner under the pile of old stuff, I found a baseball and then a glove, and in the very bottom of the pile, I found an old metal bat. Just like the kind Liam and Wes used when they were my age.

Sometimes it pays to be the little sister. My whole life I've been following Wes and Liam around hoping that they would play with me. I even told Wes that one day he would marry me. He just laughed and said, "I'm not so sure about that, Squirt." That's what he calls me. Squirt.

So, all the times, I followed them around when they played ball or walked in the woods finally is going to pay off even if Wes never wants to marry me because I learned how to swing a baseball bat watching them. I learned to run through the woods following them. I am going to run away from the bad man because of all that I watched them do.

So, I wait. And I wait, and I wai,t and I wait. I almost fall asleep. Almost. I feel my eyelids getting heavy but then I hear footsteps and I know that he's coming. He always comes.

So, I sit quietly and try not to make any noise. I hurry to my feet and grab my bat. I crouch in the corner with the bat over my shoulder just like Liam showed me how to do. When I hear the lock that he keeps on the closet door open I know that it's time.

My hands sweat, and I feel shaky all over.

"Wake up, Claire, it's time," he says as he pulls open the closet door. "What are you doing?" He asks when he sees me, but I don't answer. I swing the bat as hard as I can, hitting him in his big belly.

When the bad man falls forward, I swing one more time, hitting the side of his head just like Liam and Wes taught me to hit a baseball when I finally got them to include me. And then I run, my favorite ball cap tumbling to the floor, but I don't stop for it. I can't stop for it. I just have to run, and run, and run, and I keep running.

I run out of the closet while the bad man screams

my name. I run out of the ugly house that smells funny and then I run out into the woods.

I run, and I run, and I run. But I know he's going to catch me. A mean hand grabs me by my arm from behind and I scream . . .

chapter 24

she's gone

Wes

"SOMETHING'S WRONG," I SAY quietly. "What's taking her so long?"

Lee laughs. "Nothing is wrong. Chill out, man. Nothing is going to go wrong."

"I mean it, Lee," I say looking to my best friend since birth. I feel an edginess that only comes with years of honing a great gut instinct that has kept us both alive on more than one occasion.

After a moment, he looks at his watch again. "It has been awhile. I'll just go check on her . . ." he says before taking off down the hall.

He's taking too long. I feel it in my bones, something's wrong with Claire. I realize I was standing from the table when he calls out my name.

"Wes! Down here!" he shouts from back down the hall by the bathrooms.

Just like fucking *Cinderella*, one of her shoes, those ridiculous heels that I told her turned me on, is laying on its side. She must have dropped it on her way out.

Part of me thinks she ran, but I know that's not it. Claire wouldn't run from this, from us, she's in it one hundred percent and then some.

"She's gone." Lee echoes my thoughts. Someone took my Claire. Again. And that burns in my gut. I know deep down in my soul that whoever took her this time won't let her escape. Have her demons really come back to haunt us like this? When we are finally so close to having everything we ever wanted?

"Find anyone who saw something. Talk to everyone here. No one leaves," I demand.

"I pull my phone out of my pocket to call her, but it goes straight to voicemail. I kick myself for my stupidity. Her little green clutch with the peacock on it is still sitting by her place at the head table next to my seat with my jacket over it. I know with certainty that she didn't leave of her own accord now, but then, who took her? Only family and friends are here tonight. Who do we know that would betray us like this? That could have betrayed her twenty-four years ago?

"We're going to find her," Lee tries to reassure me and him both.

"We better, or it's going to kill me . . . Lee, there's something you don't know . . ." I start to tell him what I have suspected for a week or two now, but never brought up to Claire. I never had the courage to ask her.

"What's that?" he asks me, but I can't share my deepest thoughts and hopes with him. Not yet.

"Nothing, let's just find her," I tell him.

We head back to the dining room, but the scene is wrong. Something is different.

"Who's missing?" Lee asks.

"Holy shit," I whisper. "No." Just in time to see Lee's dad race from the building. He wouldn't betray me like this. He couldn't. The blood is rushing in my ears and my heart is about to beat out of my chest because I cannot rationalize a world where he would betray me like this. But in my head, I know that he did.

"Where were you standing in the yard the night that Claire came home?" Lee asks me.

"Facing the woods to the east," I tell him as all the pieces to our fucked-up puzzle start to fit together. The answer was right in front of my face all along. I think I'm going to be sick,

"Shit! The old neighborhood is easily an hour away," Lee says like he's about to brace me for bad news. "I think I know who took Claire,"

"Me too," I say gravely. "We better get moving."

chapter 25

it's you

Claire

THERE IS A MARCHING band pounding away in my brain.

I must have had too much to drink at the rehearsal dinner last night. I think. I better be able to get my ass ready for today—my wedding day—because if I don't, my bestie, Emma, will have my ass.

I pry my eyes open, only then do I realize that I am not in our hotel room on the coast. I'm not in the luxury king sized bed full of fluffy euro pillows and down comforters near a window looking out at the Atlantic Ocean. I'm not where I should be. It takes my brain a minute, still feeling as fuzzy as it is, to register that I'm not . . . *safe*.

The light shines through the wooden slats of the doors.

I'm here. I am right back where I started. Where I thought I would die when I was so small, just a baby really. I'm where I once escaped and had naively thought

I would never be back. I scoot back on the worn, torn carpet floor of the closet that I was locked in once before, until my back hits the wall. I try to make myself as small as possible hoping against all hope that he won't see me but as I hear the footsteps growing louder and louder, I know that there is no hope to be found at all.

The closet door swings open, and I realize how stupid I have been. All this time that I struggled, that I suffered from those terrible nightmares and prayed that they would either end or I would finally remember just who had tried to harm me when I was just six years old. All those times I thought I was safe, that I was free, were really nothing but lies because looking down at me with a sinister smile on his face in this little house of horrors from my haunted past is the last person I ever would have thought would be capable of this kind of thing.

I was never free, I was living under the watchful eye of a monster—a wolf in sheep's clothing just waiting for their chance to pounce. His smile broadens and his eyes glimmer with excitement in the knowledge that he's won. It's finally over, this game of cat and mouse that we have been silently engaged in for twenty-four years is finished.

How stupid I was. How many times did I go to dinner at their house? How many times did I think he was the one in my corner? For fucks sake, I even fell in love with his son.

He pulls his leather belt free from his pants and loops it around my neck. I look up into his warm eyes, ones that I had always trusted as he tightens the leather around my neck.

"It's you. It was always you," I say as look into the eyes so much like the ones on the face I see every night before I got to sleep. Judge O'Connell looks down at me with triumph in his brown eyes and suddenly every memory finally clicks into place.

Anna would be so proud.

I gasp as the air is squeezed out of my lungs. I struggle to pull more in even though in my brain I know that it isn't possible. Maybe this is how it was always supposed to be. Maybe this is how my story was always supposed to end. I was never supposed to get the guy. I was never supposed to get the happily ever after. I was never supposed to live . . .

Spots start to dance in front of my eyes. I keep fighting even though I don't know why. I should just relax and let destiny take me, maybe? When the door to the cabin swings open with a thud and there stand my dad, my first hero, come to save me.

"Let my daughter go, you sick fuck!" he demands, and Judge O'Connell looks nervous for a minute when my dad raises his gun. A small *Smith & Wesson* thirty-eight and loosens his hold on the belt around my neck. I can finally take a breath, shallow as it might be. "I trusted you!"

My dad pulls the hammer back and the barrel spins but before he has a chance to pull the trigger a loud boom erupts in the room and red blood blooms out around my dad's chest. His face a mask of surprise and disbelief as he crumples to the floor.

"No!" I scream. "No, no, no, no. Dad!"

I was almost safe again. My dad, my hero, he had come to rescue me and they murdered him. I can't take my eyes from where he's slumped over by the sofa. This is all my fault. My only consolation is that I won't have to look my mother in the eyes and admit my fault in everything.

"I couldn't let you win," my future mother-in-law says as she steps out of the shadows with a small pearl handled revolver in her hand. I remember the year Wes bought it for her for Christmas because he wanted her to feel safe in her own home while her husband was busy sending the bad guys to prison. And now she used it to murder my dad. What a joke.

"You couldn't let me win?" I snap. Tears burn down my face. How much more could they take from me. If this is winning, I would much rather lose. "When did I ever win?"

"You stole my husband!" she screams at me. "Did you want me to just sit back and watch while he became obsessed with you? Your dark hair and your pretty purple eyes. The pink of your mouth and the way it turned him on. I couldn't take it anymore!"

"I didn't steal your husband!" I scream right back not caring one fuck that my hands are still bound and I'm about to die too. "Your husband kidnapped me and molested me!"

"You made him do it. He couldn't help himself the way you called to him like a siren," she argues her crazy delusions and her husbands.

"I was six years old!" I yell. "I was just a baby and you took everything away from me."

"You were going to ruin everything!" she says. "My life, my husband's career, everything that we had worked so hard for was all going to fall down like a house of cards because he could not stay away from you."

"You're sick." I spit.

"So, he took you and was going to do whatever he needed to with you to get it out of his system," she says like it's no big deal.

"He was never going to let me go, was he?" I ask her.

"Of course not," she says looking at me like I was always a disappointment. "We couldn't have any loose ends walking around and talking, now could we? And then somehow you managed to escape him, but you didn't remember anything. So I thought, what's the harm?"

"So why now?" I ask her.

"Because you can't take both of my boys from me!" she screams losing the tight grip on her control again. "You can't have both my husband and my son."

"I just want Wes. I'm in love with Wes," I say strongly.

"Yes, and they are both in love with you," she sneers. "But with you back in Wes's life he will never run for office like we expect him to. Like we need him to in order to carry on the family tradition."

"Wes doesn't want that," I tell her.

"No, you don't want that. This is what Wesley was bred for. But with you hanging around, his father can't seem to get a rein on his . . . appetites." Oh gross, I think I'm going to barf. "We watched the Hunter chase you and I thought, for once luck has smiled on me and someone else will handle my dirty work, but alas, no."

"Why are you doing this?" I ask her.

"So that my husband and my son can move on, with me at their sides, of course," she answers coolly.

"Of course."

"Now, can I have her?" Judge O'Connell asks as he digs his fingers into my hair pulling some stands from my scalp when I try to flinch away. He caresses my lip with his thumb. The vomit burns in my throat and I know that I'm seconds away from puking again.

"You have one hour to play," she tells her husband. "And then I'll be back to finish the job once and for all."

Mrs. O'Connell turns to walk away but the door swings open again this time Wes is there and his face is wrenched with pain and betrayal. I want to reach out and comfort him, but I can't. His dad is holding me by my hair and my hands are still bound.

"What the actual fuck is happening here?" he roars as takes in the room.

"Wesley, leave right now," his mother orders. "I will have all of this cleaned up like it never happened. And then we can move on together, as a family."

"Are you fucking crazy?" he thunders. "You think I'll just sit back and let you murder my wife?"

"She's not your wife yet," she snaps. "And she never should be. She ruins everything. Now step back, Wesley, before I have to shoot you too."

"You would really shoot me?" he asks dumbstruck.

"I would do anything to protect your father," she says. Poor Wes, that has to hurt. "Now, let's move past this."

"No," Wes says breaking my heart. "Dad, let her go."

"I can't, Wesley," he admits. "I need her more than you could ever understand."

"No, Dad," Wes says. "Because I need her so much that I can't live without her."

"I'm sorry, Wesley," he says not even looking up to his son as he answers. Instead he's watching my eyes as he slowly pulls on the tail of his belt and squeezes the air out of my body.

"No!" he shouts as the room explodes.

Liam and Surfer push through the door and into the room. They both fire guns in their hands. Who shot who, I still can't tell. But Judge and Mrs. O'Connell are gone and for that I am truly grateful and also heartbroken for Wes. I'm not sure we can move on from this. If my kidnapper was anyone else, I think we would be fine, but a betrayal like that from his parents will cut deep.

"I knew you'd get here in time, Son," my dad's voice wraps in the room.

"Dad!" Lee and I both shout.

"I'm not out yet," he says. "I have too much life to live still." And thank God for that.

Wes comes over and pulls a folding knife out of his pocket and without saying a word, he cuts the ties that bind my hands together and pulls his father's belt from around my neck. And then he turns and walks outside without saying another word.

The sirens sing in the distance and I know that the police are on the way. It's a huge relief but at the same time, I am worried about Wes. My heart breaks for him.

My dad was whisked away in an ambulance but this time the medics said he looked good and that it was good that he was talking. So I didn't go running after him into the night like I did with Jones, plus I knew I had to stay and give all the statements.

It's hard to lay my soul bare and put all my demons on display for my fellow officers to see but I do. I give my statement and I tell them everything. Lee and Surfer give statements as well because they discharged weapons but we all know that the shoots will be clean upon review. And then in an interesting plot twist, some men in black show up and whisk Surfer away after demanding that his entire statement be retracted because he was never here.

"Whoa," I say after they leave.

"You have no idea," Lee says his eyes wide. "I had heard, but, yeah, whoa sums it up."

"I have no idea what just happened," I tell my brother.

"I think for both our sakes we should pretend it didn't," he tells me. "You going to be okay, kiddo?"

"I think so," I say. "I'm not sure though. The jury is still out."

"I think you'll be alright," he says after a minute. "But that one needs you bad."

My eyes follow Lee's down the gravel drive to where Wes is standing with his shoulder slumped and his head hanging low.

"He hasn't said a word to me, Lee," I admit. "I'm worried he can't look at me anymore."

"He feels guilty," Lee tells me. "Like it's all his fault that you got hurt. Then and now."

"But it's not," I say.

"Don't tell me that." Lee shrugs. "Tell him.

"I think I'll do just that," I say as I push up from where Lee and I were sitting and walk over to Wes.

I press my front to his back and wrap myself around his waist. His arms wrap around mine locking me to him.

"I am so very fucking sorry, baby," he starts.

"You have nothing to be sorry for," I say with all honestly. "You saved me, then and now."

"I didn't," he says shaking his head. "Surfer shot my dad, although we can never tell anyone that."

"I know," I tell him. "Lee and I got the shake down from the men in black too. It was wild."

"I told you to leave him alone," he says softly.

"Lee said he'd heard a rumor . . ." I trail off.

"I know more than Lee," he tells me and when I open my mouth, he stops me. "But I still won't tell you."

"Damn it, Wes!" I pout.

"Do you think you can still love me?" he asks me quietly. Wes's vulnerability cuts me to the quick.

"I have loved you since I was six years old and you gave me your ball cap," I tell him honestly. "And I have never stopped, and I never will."

Wes pulls me around to face him and crushes his lips down on mine in a soul searing kiss. Wes and I might have a rocky road in front of us, but it's nothing we can't handle because life with Wes is always worth it.

"Wanna get married?" I ask him.

"Probably right after you get checked out at the hospital," he tells me.

"I'm fine," I deny any injury.

"About that," he says as he runs his finger tip across the bruises on my neck that have been purpling deeper and deeper over the last hour. "I think there are some things we should have checked out."

chapter 26

the one

One Week Later . . .

"ARE YOU READY FOR your forever?" Emma asks me as she pulls my simple veil over my head.

"Yeah," I smile. "I was born ready."

"Then let's do this!" she cheers making me laugh.

Emma kisses my cheek through the thin material before herding my nieces out through the French doors on the patio. I hear the first strings of the song that they are walking down the aisle to and I know that this is it. There are no more hurdles to jump. I can finally be with Wes.

This is the first day of the rest of our lives.

The music changes and it's *The Longer the Wait, The Sweeter the Kiss* by Josh Turner and it couldn't be more fitting. Wes and I have literally waited our whole lives to get here.

This is my cue. The French doors open one more time and I step out to look up into the face of my brother, Liam, who is smiling sweetly at me and looking very handsome in his Navy dress blues. A uniform that I haven't seen in a very long time and still holds a special spot in my heart.

"Wes and I got permission to wear them," he says noticing what has my attention. I smile at him.

"What are you doing here?" I ask him. He is supposed to be standing at the altar with Wes as his best man but instead he's here, surprising me.

"What?" he asks on a wink. "Can't a guy give his only sister away to his best friend?"

"I guess a guy could if that guy is you," I say softly feeling a little choked up.

Lee walks me through the courtyard garden path that winds its way down to the sea where Wes and everyone else are waiting for us. At the front of the aisle waits my dad.

Lee hands me over to my dad who turns to Lee and says, "I've got it from here."

"I know you do, Dad," Lee says. "But mind if I tag along?"

"Sounds great, Son," my dad says to Lee before turning to me. "Sorry about the sling, your mother wouldn't let me skip it."

I can't help but bark out a laugh. We are all so much alike. That Goodnite stubbornness is a sight to behold.

"I'm sure it's fine, Dad," I tell him. "Hey, we've got matching father-daughter gunshot wounds."

"That's not funny," Dad and Lee growl at the same time making me smile even brighter.

"I always knew that Wes was the one," Dad says to me and emotion clogs my throat. "Treat each other with kindness and love."

"I will," I promise my dad.

"I know you will."

When we reach the altar, Wes is waiting with a smile on his face like I have never seen before and if I'm not mistake, a shimmer in his eye that matches mine. I'm barely holding on to my emotions. I'm going to cry like a little baby and we all know it.

"Remember what I said, Wesley," my dad says to him as he passes my hand from his to Wes's.

"Yes, Sir, I do," Wes answers and Lee smirks.

"Who gives this woman away?" the minister asks.

"Her mother and I do," my dad answers.

"Thank you. You may be seated."

"I wouldn't give her to anyone but you, Brother," Lee says to Wes as he takes his place beside him and pats him on the shoulder like men do.

"I know," Wes answers and the emotion in his voice is telling.

"What did my dad say to you that was so important?" I whisper to Wes as the minister begins the ceremony.

"No take backs," he whispers back. I can't help the smile that spreads across my face and I barely restrain my laughter.

That is so like my dad to welcome Wes to the family officially and then tell him no take backs. I come from a family of weirdos and I wouldn't have it any other way. And at the same time, Dad is providing Wes with the family that he always deserved and didn't get.

"Marriage is not a shelter for the faint of heart," the minister begins. "But I believe you two already know that one."

He is an older man with a kind smile and white hair. His stature is small, but his presence is huge. When we explained our situation to him last week and why would couldn't have a priest or a judge, he said he would be happy to perform our marriage ceremony.

"At this time, the best man will perform a Navy tradition, and ring a ships bell for each of the important people in the Bride and Groom's lives that are no longer with us and could not be here today," he says before calling out each name.

"Officer Luis Rodriguez." Lee rings the big brace bell once.

"Officer Matt Jerome." Lee rings the bell twice.

"Officer Jasmine Alexander." Lee rings the bell a third time.

"The bride's sister, Bonnie." Lee rings the bell a fourth time and I know what's coming so I take a deep breath a steel myself. Wes takes my hand in his giving me a gentle squeeze of support.

"And their dear friend, Anna Parker." Lee rings the bell a fifth time and I look over my shoulder to the chair on the aisle that was left open for her with her bouquet sitting on top of it and offer up a silent prayer that wherever Anna is, that she is happy.

"At this time, Wesley and Claire have chosen to recite their own vows."

"Wes, I promise to make you feel loved and cherished every day. I promise not to drive you too crazy, only a little crazy. I'll be your shelter in the storm as you have been mine. I will not stop making fun of your Fed suits or your Fed-mobile because we both know you secretly like it. I won't promise to be perfect, but I promise to love you with all that I am until the day that I die. This is my vow," I say softly.

"Claire, I have always loved you. In fact, I can't remember a time when I didn't in one way or another. I promise to be your lover and protector. I promise to be your shelter in the storm the way that you have been mine. I promise not to overly judge your disgusting love of junk food but will continue to appreciate the ass that it provides you."

"Wes!"

"I will love you and honor you faithfully until the day I die. This is my vow," he continues his voice ringing loud and true.

"I now pronounce you husband and wife. You may kiss the bride," the minister finishes loudly to the shouts and whistles and catcalls of all the SEALs including Surfer.

I look to Wes and smile as he flips my veil over my face and pulls me into his arms. Wes kisses my socks off, that is if I was wearing socks and not these ridiculous heels Emma made me get.

"Ready?" he asks me.

"To be with you?"

"Yeah," he smiles at me.

"I was born ready." And then he takes my hand and we get started on the first day of the rest of our lives.

By the time we walk into the reception hall my cheeks hurt from smiling but I am ecstatic at the idea that when Wes and I get back from our honeymoon in Italy that we will have a stack of pictures to put up in our house and one day show our children.

The room is filled with all of our friends and family who cheer ridiculously loud when Wes and I are introduced as Mr. and Mrs. O'Connell. I'm pretty sure it was the SEALs. They are a pretty rowdy bunch even in their early forties.

Mr. and Mrs. O'Connell.

I have to admit. I love the sound of it. I'll probably always be Goody or Detective Goodnite at work, but in real life, I am Claire O'Connell. I know that Wes thinks that after everything that happened that I wouldn't want to take his family name, but in truth I want to be tied to Wes in as many ways as possible.

My love for him is that big.

Wes leads me out into the middle of the dance floor and twirls me into his arms. We dance under the lights to the words of Yours by Russell Dickerson and they couldn't be more true. Wes expertly twirls me around the dance floor.

I have lived many years before Wes came back into my life, but with him I can accomplish anything, I can survive whatever life throws at me because I have him by my side. He truly makes my life better in every way.

"Thank God I'm yours," Wes repeats the song lyrics in my ear as the song ends.

"I thank God I'm yours too, Wes." The tears still shimmer in his eyes. Mine too. I knew today would be full of feeling but I love it. My heart is full to bursting for him.

My love for him is that big.

"It's time," Wes says to me later that evening.

There is one last thing to do and I am dreading it, but it needs to be done. It's time to say goodbye to my friend.

Emma, Lee, Wes and I quietly leave the party and walk out to the beach barefoot. We carry nothing with us but Anna's bouquet.

Side by side we stand in the dark with the waves crashing over our feet as we silently offer each other support as we say goodbye one last time.

"Thank you for a beautiful day, Anna. I miss you," I say out loud.

"Thank you for being my friend. I miss you," Emma says. Her tears leave tracks down her face.

"I wish you peace, Anna," Wes says.

"Be free," Lee adds last before I toss her bouquet into the ocean,

"Goodbye, Fancy Pants," I say. "Until we meet again."

"Emma, can we talk?" Lee asks as she turns to walk away.

"Has hell frozen over yet?" she snaps back. Her emotions are obviously riding her hard right now as she wars between wanting Lee and her guilt over Anna.

"It doesn't have to be like this," he says softly. She

looks like she waivers for a split second before walking off.

"It does," she calls over her shoulder.

"This is ridiculous," he barks as he trails off after her.

"She feels guilty," Wes says wrapping me up in his arms. "Don't worry, Lee's a tenacious guy. He'll figure it out."

"That's what I'm worried about," I tell him.

We stand there looking out at the sea with me cradled protectively in his arms. Wes silently giving me the comfort that I need to know that everything is going to be alright.

Because his love for me is that big.

"It's time to cut the cake," the wedding planner tells us after we return to the reception.

She herds us toward a massive cake that is as tall as I am sitting on the table. On top of the cake is a small statue of the VJ day kiss couple and I love it. It's a little scandalous and I just know that this was Emma's contribution. The rest of the cake starts in a deep pink at the bottom and fades up to white at the top in the most beautiful ombre. It's very classy.

I place my hand on top of Wes's on the cake knife and together, we slide out a small piece. I scoop it up with the server and put it on a plate to hand to Wes.

"It's chocolate," he says surprised to see the rich

color of the actual cake.

"Yeah, I know," I tell him. "It's your favorite."

"You got my favorite cake for our wedding cake?" he asks me.

"Well, yeah," I answer his question. "I wanted you to have special things today too."

I don't get a chance to finish that train of thought because Wes, so moved with love and the spirit of today, that he pulls me into his body and crushes his mouth to mine in a kiss even better than our wedding kiss. As his tongue sweeps into my mouth the rest of the room falls away and I am lost to Wes.

That is until the room erupts with cheers and whistles and I have to duck my head to hide the embarrassment stinging my cheeks. Wes just laughs.

"Maybe we should put a pin in that thought," I say for his ears only making Wes laugh even harder.

"Sure, baby. Whatever you say."

He scoops up a small bite on one of the forks and offers it to me. I keep my eyes on his as I open my mouth and take his offer. I hold a bite out for Wes and he just shakes his head no. I roll my eyes letting him know that this isn't part of the agenda.

He just laughs and kisses me again.

"I prefer my cake from your lips," he says wiping the corner of his mouth.

"You are incorrigible," I tell him on a laugh.

"Better get used to it, baby." But I hope I never get used to it. I hope I wake up every day for the rest of my life with the overwhelming feeling that I am incredibly blessed. That I am the luckiest woman in the world because Wes makes me feel that way every day.

Because his love for me is just that big.

Emma

A little Dutch courage is going to be my downfall.

I could see the toasts coming a mile away like a bad car crash on the turnpike. I knew that Lee was going to be charming when he gave his. I also knew that I was sorely unprepared to see him in his old Navy dress blues. Dear baby Jesus in a trench coat it should be illegal for a man to look that good in a uniform.

So, I was nervous and all through dinner the champagne was free flowing. I partook of that champagne. And then I realized shortly after I gave my toast—one that was free of all the delightful stories of Wes's penis because my bestie, Claire, can be a little dull from time to time—that I had perhaps imbibed too much.

My face felt flushed, my body felt hot, and I knew that I needed some fresh air. So, after I wished my bestie and her groom a long and happy life of blissful joy and boning—and real talk, I killed it in there—I excused myself from the party to go back to the water's edge to catch my breath and cool down. What I didn't plan on was a very sexy police Captain, one I can't seem to keep my hands off of, had followed me.

"You can't avoid me forever," he says softly from just behind me.

"It would be a lot easier if you played along," I

whine just a little bit. God damnit, I am a strong and independent woman, I do not like how needy I am around this one man.

"I can't do that, baby," he says. "I need you too much."

"No," I deny.

"And I think you need me too," his sexy voice rumbles and I feel it in a lot of interesting places, but then again, with Lee I always do.

"No," I whisper.

"And I think you're scared to fall," he says softly as he puts his hands on my shoulders and gently turns me around to face him. "But I'll catch you, I promise."

"What if you don't?" I ask ashamed to admit how scared I am.

"You have to trust me," he says.

"I can't."

"Just for tonight," Lee pleads. "Just trust me for tonight and we'll go from there."

"Okay," I say softly.

"Okay?" he asks unsure of what to do now that I have agreed.

"Okay," I repeat.

He looks so happy and I'm half afraid that it's the champagne that's making me agree to be his even if it's only for a night. No, that's a lie. Truth be told, I am in love with Liam Goodnite, and just as much as I know that he is it for me, I also know that I could never hold him. A man like Lee would get tired of being with one woman after a while, especially if that woman is me. I know that it hurts like hell to walk away now, but it would kill me to see him walking away after six months or a year of loving him the way that I would if I could bring myself to let down my guard.

I look up and realize that we have slowly moved out of the light shining from the reception and down to just under the pier. It's dark here and a little secluded. The music from the party can be barely heard.

And in that moment, I want Lee like I have never wanted anything in my life.

"Don't look at me like that, Emma," he says his voice strained. "I can't walk away like a gentleman when you look at me like that."

"Like what?" I ask.

"Like you want me. Like you need my cock like you need air to breath. Like you want me to make that pretty pink pussy of yours come," he says his voice low and rumbly.

"Yes," I breathe as I back up and my shoulders hit one of the wooden posts of the pier. "I want that. All of it."

"Emma," he pleads as he says my name like a prayer.

"I want that," I say letting the wine make me bolder than I normally would be. "I want your cock and I want you to make me come. And I want you."

"Fuck," he bites out before crashing his mouth down on mine.

Lee kisses me like a drowning man in a hurricane, his kiss is fierce and powerful and all consuming. I let out a whimper and he takes that opportunity to sweep his tongue inside my mouth and I suck it deep letting it brush over mine as he plunges it in and out of my mouth.

He breaks his mouth away from mine and I miss it immediately.

"Lee," I plead. What for, I'm not sure, I just know that I need more. More of his kisses, more of his touch on my skin, his cock. I don't know. I just need more.

Slowly, so painfully slowly, Lee slides the skirt of my dress up bunching it in his large hand as he goes. When it's up above my hips, exposing my delicate pink panties, Lee slides the damp material aside and plunges two fingers into my pussy.

"So wet for me," he says softly.

"Yes," I agree. I lean my weight back on the post as my knees begin to buckle.

"Are you going to come for me like this or do you want my cock in that pretty pussy of yours?" he asks me. And I will con on his hand if he keeps it up, but tonight I'm giving into all the vices that are bad for my health: wine, Lee, and if he fucks my brains out I'll go bum a smoke from one of the valet guys.

"I want your cock," I say honestly. I watch captivated as he unbuttons the front of his trousers. His hard length springs free and I want it. I want all of it. Everything that Lee has to give me. In this moment, I will take whatever that may be. No regrets, I will YOLO the fuck out of him.

"That's my girl." Oh, how I wish I were his girl. God what would it be like to be loved by him like that. "Lift your leg around my hip. That's it."

He pulls the gusset of my panties to the side and slides his cock all the way in. Lee lifts me up, bracing his hands under my ass so that he can lift me up and the drive me down on his cock over and over again.

"Oh God," I moan as he slides me up so that only the tip is inside me and then powers me back down again.

"That's it," he says as I clench around him as he slides me up and then drives me down on him again.

"I-I'm going to—" I gasp as my orgasm rolls over me like a steamroller. "Lee!

He pins me to the post and pumps once, twice more before calling out my name into the night as he follows me over the edge. "Emma!"

Lee holds me in his arms against the wooden post as we both struggle to catch our breaths. He leans his forehead against mine.

"So, what are you doing for the rest of tonight?" he asks me.

"I had grand plans to go bum a smoke from one of the valet guys," I admit and feel Lee's smile against my mouth.

"Well, seeing as how they have all gone home for the night, how about you come back to my room with me instead?"

"I suppose I could do that instead," I say hesitantly.

"Excellent," he whispers.

Lee sets me on my feet and waits for me to regain my balance and then hand in hand we walk down the beach and back up to the resort where Lee will let us in his room and we'll spend another night together.

What could one more night hurt?

Claire

Fireworks of all colors burst bright overhead.

It's midnight and one of the last fireworks displays of the season. Most of our guests have gone home or to their rooms in the resort and only a few stragglers are left. Wes and I wanted to enjoy the entire night instead of rushing out to be alone. This wedding felt like a long time in the making and we wanted to enjoy all of it.

"Look at that one!" I point to a big purple firework that glitters in the sky. "It's so pretty."

"Not as pretty as you," he whispers.

"Wes," I smile feeling a little shy at all of the attention today.

Wes wraps his arms around me and I lean my back to his front and enjoy the rest of the fireworks show, that is until he presses his erection into my ass and it's hard enough that I can feel it through the miles and miles of froth fabric that my dress consists of.

"Have I told you yet how much I love this dress?" Wes leans down and rumbles in my ear.

"No, I don't believe you have yet," I tell him.

"Well, I do believe it's about time that I sing its praises."

"As you should," I agree.

"You ready to get out of her, Mrs. O'Connell?" he asks me.

"For life with you?" I answer him with a big smile on my face. "I was born ready."

And then Wes and I sneak out and head up to our honeymoon suite that overlooks the ocean to get started on the rest of our forever. One thing I'm sure of, life with Wes will never be boring. I can't wait.

epic epilogue

the best day of my life

Claire
6 weeks later . . .

"ARE YOU READY FOR this?" I ask Wes as we walk out of the doctor's office and jump in his car. As always, Wes holds the door open for me, ever the gentleman.

"Of course," he answers smoothly. "Why would you think I wouldn't be?"

"Well, you were looking a little green around the gills there. I thought we might be puking together for a second there."

"I never puke," my husband says with all seriousness.

All this talk of vomit has my stomach turning. Long gone are the days of my waking up to be sick because of the lasting effects of a nightmare that wouldn't let me go, and now I puke regularly for a whole new reason. A great reason. I'm pregnant.

Wes and I are having a baby.

"Let's stop talking about puking, please," I say my voice a little high and uncomfortable. Wes gives me a knowing smirk, but fortunately changes the subject.

We are on our way to meet Emma and Lee for lunch to tell them the good news and to officially move me to desk duty and filing. Yay! Not really, while I know that I will be bored off of my ass for the next six months, I know that it is what I need to do, so I'm finally okay with being benched.

Tonight at dinner, we're going to tell my mom and dad.

Wes had started suspecting that big changes were on the horizon the week before I was taken again, and he had even planned to talk to me that night about it. It turns out my husband is a very perceptive man because he was right.

The directions we forgot to read after I was shot by The Hunter had neglected to inform us that the antibiotic shot that I was given in the hospital and the prescription that I was given for oral antibiotics after I was discharged had rendered my birth control shot completely ineffective. I had no idea and now I'm glad for it because I couldn't be happier.

Wes pulls into the parking lot of the diner around the corner from the station. Neither Lee or Emma's cars are here. And I'm sad to admit that they are not together after our wedding. I had high hopes that they would finally work their problems out, but I guess it just isn't meant to be.

Wes holds the shiny glass door open for me and holds up his hands to ask for a four top. The hostess grabs four menus before walking us to a table just around the corner from the dessert counter and suddenly I am ravenous.

I open my menu, and everything looks good but I hone in on the double bacon cheeseburger. When I look up, Emma and Lee are headed our way.

"Hey!" I say jumping up to hug my best friend and my big brother.

"So, how was the honeymoon?" Lee asks.

"Italy was amazing," Wes says with a smug smirk on his face.

"Oh, gross," Lee says making a gagging noise. "That's my sister, asshole."

"No, that is my very sexy wife."

"Ok, that was kind of gross, Wes," I tell him.

"Too far?" he asks playfully.

"Just a smidge," I say holding up my thumb and index fingers about an inch apart.

"My apologies," he says on a not at all feeling guilty smile.

The waitress comes and takes our order and I settle on the double cheeseburger and extra fries. Emma asks for chicken noodle soup, but she just pushes it around in her bowl. Come to think of it she's not looking that great. I feel bad, but I also don't want to catch anything if it's contagious.

"Are you feeling alright?" I ask her softly for her ears only but then Lee hones in on what I've said.

"Are you sick?" he asks.

"I'm fine," she answers but the look on her face says she's anything but. "So, what did you call us down here to tell us?"

I lean back in my seat and look at Wes before answering. "I'm pregnant."

"No shit," Lee laughs. "I thought you were just fat."

"You asshole," I grumble while Wes laughs. "Why do I like you again?"

"Because I'm your favorite big brother," he explains.

"You are my only big brother," I correct him.

"And I'm really happy for you, kiddo," he tells me. "But for real, you are looking kind of fat."

"Nice knowing you," Wes mumbles but I choose to ignore that.

"I'm not fat, you nut sack! I'm having twins," I shout.

Emma looks around a little uncomfortable before seizing her opportunity to escape. "I guess I'm not feeling well after all, I should go," she says before tossing a twenty on the table and practically running for the door.

"What was that all about?" I ask Lee.

He lets out a heavy sigh. "I just don't know. We were fine until about a week ago and then she just stopped calling and started looking really sad again. I can't get her to talk to me."

"Well, I'm sure you'll figure it out," I try to reassure my brother.

"I will," he tells me. "Don't worry about me. I'm happy for you guys."

"Thanks, Lee," Wes says shaking his hand as my brother stands and drops a twenty on the table. He walks out of the diner and I have a funny feeling he's going to go after Emma. Again.

"Ready to get out of here?" Wes asks me throwing some more cash on the pile on the table.

"Yes, but first I need pie," I tell him.

"One celebratory piece of pie to go," he tells me as he stands to make his way over to the dessert counter.

"Better make it two if you want any because I'm not sharing," I inform my better half.

"This pregnancy has only made your eating habits worse," he tells me. "At some point in time you are going to have to eat a vegetable."

"Bite your tongue!" I laugh.

"Pie coming right up," he says as he returns with my pie.

Wes leads me out to the car where he drives me back to our house.

"Do you want your pie now or later, baby?" he asks me as he lets us into the house.

"Later," I tell him. "Now I kind of just want to hang out with you."

"Sure," he says. "What do you want to do?"

"Watch a movie with me?" I shrug. We almost never have down time, but I got used to just being lazy with Wes in Italy.

"Sure," he says as we snuggle up on the sofa with a big throw blanket. "Maybe we'll find a sexy highlander for you."

"Oh, you're so funny," I play swat him. Wes still teases me about the romance novels my mom gave when I was recovering from being shot and they still lead to some pretty steamy moments with my guy.

"I'm just teasing," he tells me as he brushes a lock of my hair back from my face. "I love you, Claire."

"And I love you," I tell him.

"Never stop saying it," he says softly. "I need the words."

"I'll always love you."

We sit on the couch and watch some spy movie that we have both seen a thousand times. It will probably always remind me of the night that the men in black came for one of my husband's friends. But as we promised each other that night, we have never spoke of it again.

We also haven't seen Surfer since the wedding.

After a while I ask, "Are you really happy?"

"Of course," Wes says turning to face me. "Why wouldn't I be?"

"I don't know," say fidgeting suddenly feeling a little insecure. Fucking hormones. "It happened so fast. I just don't want you to regret anything."

"Look at me, baby," Wes says lifting my chin to meet his eyes. "I have not one regret when it comes to be married to you. I want these babies with every fiber of my being and I love you just as much. So, don't be nervous. Be happy and enjoy this time with me before we're a four."

"Okay," I say finally letting myself feel truly happy.

"And baby," he says.

"Yeah?"

"One more thing. This is by far, the best day of my life."

Wes

6 months later . . .

"I'm here!" I shout as I race through the hospital. "I'm here. I'm here!"

"Right this way, Mr. O'Connell. They're waiting on you," the nurse tells me. "Put on these scrubs and then come with me." She shoves me into a changing room and I dress as fast as I can.

When I jump out of the room she's standing there waiting for me and she has a look on her face like I'm the biggest screw up she's ever seen.

The nurse leads me down a long hallway and pulls me into an Operating Room that looks like it's something out of an Alien Abduction Sci-Fi movie. There are huge circular lights overhead and the love of my life is draped over a steel table in the middle of the room. She's surrounded by people in scrubs and rubber gloves and surgical masks. The nurse hands me a mask and a hat and shoves me in the room.

"I'm here, baby," I say as I head over to where her face is because as they are setting up a big blue paper tent, I am sure that I do not want to see my wife turned inside out.

"Glad you could make it, Dad," the surgeon says. He's a funny guy and by funny, I mean he's a raging asshole but everyone says he's the best at delivering babies so here we are. By we, I mean me as I am the one that eats all the shit he shovels my way.

"Sorry," I say eating up a little more shit. Yum! Yum! "We had a huge break on a human trafficking ring and I didn't know my wife's water was going to break while eating some Mu Shu Chicken when I was in an interrogation room." Whoops guess I'm not eating as much shit as I thought today.

"It's okay," my sweet wife says. "You're here now, that's all that matters."

"You can sit here by me," the Anesthesiologist says to me.

I think I may have impressed him by accidentally mouthing off to the doctor. But in all fairness this case is riding me pretty hard and my favorite partner has been benched for a few months. Not to mention Lee is an absolute disaster these days. But who can blame him what with everything going on in his life and all.

"Thank you," I tell him as I sit on the tiniest stool known to man. This shit wasn't made for a man of my size.

"I'm ready to meet the babies," Claire says to me. "How about you?"

"You know I have been ready for months," I tell her on a smile she can't see because it's hidden by a mask.

"We're ready to begin," the doctor says. "You're going to feel a little tugging."

"Oh," she says. "I s-s-see what you mean."

"Would you like to see your son be born?" the doctor asks and even though I know what it means I'm about to see I nod my head. "Well, stand up and say hello."

I stand, and my knees feel weak as I watch this tiny little creature all covered in crap be pulled out of my wife. It's actually kind of creepy and not at all magical but this is my boy, so I feel a burning in my nose and I know that I'm going to cry.

"We need suction," the nurse says.

"Suction."

"Take him to the NICU now!" someone shouts.

"No," I say not fully understanding what's going on. "He's supposed to come here. My wife wants the blue sheet picture. She's been saying that for months."

"Sir, your son isn't breathing we have to take him." I'm numb. I just nod and sit down on the stool.

"Wes," Claire asks. "What's going on?"

"Everything is going to be just fine," I lie. I'm not sure of anything right now. I just know that I'm numb.

"Here comes baby number two," the doctor says, and I pop up to watch a little girl with jet black hair be pulled from her mother.

Again, the nurse says, "We need suction." And my heart sinks.

"Suction."

"Be ready to transport to NICU now!" Someone shouts.

"My wife didn't even get to see them," I say as the nurses in the room gather up my baby girl and start running out of the room with her in their arms when they hear me, they *Lion King* her over their heads like that damn monkey so we can see her on the way out the door.

"Wes?" Claire says.

"Yeah, baby, I'm right here."

"I don't feel so good," she says and when I look at her she doesn't look good at all. "I think I'm going to be sick."

"Wow," the doctor says. "That is a lot of blood."

"Suction," someone calls. There's that fucking word again. I don't think I'm ever going to be able to hear it again after today.

"Sir," a nurse says. "You need to come with me to the nursery."

"No, my in-laws are there to be with the babies. I'm going to stay with my wife," I explain our plan for this delivery that they should fucking know by now because we have had it in place the entire time.

"No, Sir," she says firmly. "You have to come with me now." She starts pulling on me and I don't know what to do.

"Wes," Claire says groggily. It sounds like she's drunk. "Where are you going? What's happening?"

An alarm starts to sound in the room and the anesthesiologist says, "She's crashing."

"Sir, we have to go now!"

And I blindly follow her out of the operating room and wonder if on what would have been the happiest day of my life, did I just lose everything?

I go to the nursery and watch my beautiful little babies all cleaned up and looking so much like their mother with black hair and violet eyes. My boy's chest sucks all the way down to his spine with every breath he struggles to take and watching him guts me with every breath but how much time will I have with him? I just don't know.

My father-in-law comes in the room and pats me on the shoulder. Lee isn't here anymore but I'm not sure where he's gone off to. He's got a lot going on though, so this is the norm for him lately.

"How are you holding up?" Claire's dad asks me.

"Not so good," I mumble.

"I have to believe that it's all going to be okay," he says to me. "Our family has lost too much."

"I thought when I got the call from Lee that today, I would leave here a married father of two and there was a minute there that I wasn't sure if I would be going home a widower," I admit.

"I know," he says. "They scared the shit out of me too today. But everything will be okay, you just wait."

"I can't lose her," I voice my biggest fears.

"You won't," he reassures me. "You just have to have a little faith.

"Okay," I tell him.

"Mr. O'Connell you can see your wife in recovery now," a nurse says the sweetest words that I have ever heard to me and I jump ready to run.

"We'll just head out," he tells me as he signals to his wife that it's time to leave.

"See you in the morning," I say to them on a smile for the first time in hours

The nurse holds open a door for me and I walk into an open room with lots of beds in it, but I only have eyes for the dark-haired angel staring at me like she's never seen me before.

"You don't look so good, Wes," she says, and her voice is rough. The must have tubed her when she was sedated.

"You scared me, baby," I tell her.

"I scared myself."

"Don't ever do that to me again," I beg. I'm not afraid to be a pussy in this moment because I can't live without her. I love my wife just that much.

"I won't. How are the babies?"

"Beautiful," I tell her. "A girl and a boy."

"I'd like to name the girl Anna," she says softly.

"I like that," I tell her. "How about Faith for a middle name?"

"I like that," Claire says on a smile. "How did you come up with that?"

"Upstairs I was scared, and your dad told me I just had to have a little faith," I tell her. "Is that too cheesy?"

"Not at all. I love it. Anna Faith O'Connell," she says testing it out.

"I'd kind of like to name the boy after Lee and your dad," I tell her.

"I think they would love that," she tells me.

"But not a first name so when Lee has a kid there aren't seventy-five Liam's in the family."

"How about a middle name then?" she asks me.

"Sounds good to me."

"Wesley Liam O'Connell sounds good to me too." She kisses me sweetly. Tears clog my throat.

"You want to name our son after me?" I ask her.

"Of course," she says like it's no big deal. "You're the greatest guy I know."

"I love you," I tell her.

"And I love you," she says. "Are you happy?"

"Of course," I tell her. "Today is by far the best day of my life." To that she just smiles.

Wes

Nine months later . . .

"Beer?" my father-in-law asks me.

"Thank you, Sir," I tell him as I accept the bottle he brought over to me.

We are standing on the edges of the party while my wife and her mother are fawning over their grandchildren. Claire is sitting in an armchair with Anna Faith bouncing on her lap and I swear to Christ she has never looked more beautiful.

Her long black hair is swept up in a bun on top of her head because my son loves to cling to it and these days those bright purple eyes shine with laughter and a genuine happiness, not because of shadows that lurk in the corners of her mind.

We're at her parents' home surrounded by their friends and family because it is their fortieth anniversary. I look at them and they are so happy and still so in love and I want that. Even though I know that I don't deserve it.

I always wonder when I'm surrounded by all of the Goodnites if they hate me because I'm the product of monsters. The very same ones that lurked around every corner for their daughter.

"Thank you for letting me be part of your family," I tell him. I swallow past the lump in my throat.

"You were always part of this family, Wes." He pulls his brows together in though.

"Thank you for showing me what a normal one looks like anyways," I say letting my guard down. "I needed it more than I thought I did."

"I always knew."

"You did?" I ask him. I have to admit, that stings a little bit to know that my father-in-law always knew that my family was a colossal shit show. That I needed the Goodnites because I was being raised by wolves in sheep's clothing.

"I always knew what kind of man you'd be," he says continuing to turn my world upside down. "You and Claire have this. One day you'll look back, surrounded by grown children and grandbabies and you'll know exactly what this feels like and let me tell you, Son, it's so much more than great. It's a heat in your chest and a burning in your gut. It's the knowledge that you are the luckiest man alive and that God has seen fit to grant you so much more than you ever asked for, so much more than you ever thought you deserved."

"I know that feeling, Sir," I tell him honestly. "I feel it every morning when I look at your daughter and our children."

"Like I said before," he winks at me. "I always knew what kind of man you are." And the he walks over to Claire to claim his granddaughter out of her arms.

Claire walks over to me with a smile on her gorgeous face. "What were you and Dad talking about?" she asks me.

"How important family is," I tell her.

"I'm sorry," she says. "This kind of stuff must be hard for you."

"Not at all, baby," I smile at here. "Every day with you is easy."

"So you're happy today?" she asks me and as I think on today with my wife and our children while we celebrate her parents lifelong happiness, her dad making sure that I knew that I already was part of this family for a long time and always would be, but more importantly, that he thinks Claire and I have this kind of love, that all this beauty is my future ignites that warmth in my chest that he spoke about. I know that I already have a life of beauty with Claire as my partner, so I answer her the only way I can.

"Of course," I tell her. "Today was the best day of my life."

Wes

Christmas, six years later . . .

"Santa came! Santa came!" my beautiful kids shout as the run through the house in a whirlwind of wrapping paper and bows leaving the detritus in their wake.

"I see that!" I tell them. "Merry Christmas, kiddos."

"Merry Christmas, Wes," Claire says from beside me. We've been sipping our morning coffee while we watch the kids revel in Christmas joy.

"Merry Christmas, baby." I lean down, and I kiss her lips. Claire gets more beautiful every day and I am the lucky bastard that gets to love her.

This year the kids have grown by leaps and bounds. We've both cut back at work so that we can be at all the class parties and field trips. This year, I even coached a baseball team and it was awesome.

I couldn't ask for more.

"Looks like he brought something for daddy too," she says softly with a happy twinkle in her eyes. What could my girl be up to now? She and the kids already gave me a new baseball glove to play catch with the kids and I gave her a swing for the porch, so we can sit out there and watch the kids play together.

What could be left?

"Oh he did, did he?" I ask on a raised brow. She loves when I do that.

Claire hands me a small decorate box with a big bow on it that I definitely did not see under the tree this morning. That means she must have been hiding it somewhere to save it for last. I know then that this must be special. And when I pull the lid off the box I know that I'm right.

"Again?" I ask her feeling my heart rate pick up. In the small box was a long white stick with a big purple plus sign right in the middle and a glossy grainy picture no bigger than the palm of my hand but it holds a key component that my heart didn't know that I was missing all along.

"It's just one this time," she assures me, but it doesn't matter if it's one or five I'm still going to worry and I'm still the happiest man alive. "Are you happy?"

"Of course, baby. This is the best day of my life."

Claire

Nineteen years later . . .

"Happy Anniversary, baby," Wes says as he wraps his arms around me from behind. "What are you doing over here?"

"Just taking it all in," I answer.

Today is our twenty fifth wedding anniversary and Wes insisted we hosted all of our family and friends for a big dinner party, so our home is filled with all the people we love, Jones and his family, Lee and his. Our sister, Bonnie's kids who aren't kids anymore and their families. Hell, even our kids aren't babies anymore and the proof of that is the baby boy with black hair and violet eyes that our daughter, Anna Faith, is bouncing in her lap.

"I am a grandmother. When did that happen?" I ask my still handsome husband. His dark hair is mostly silver now and I love it. His whiskey eyes smile almost every day now.

"About six months ago," he says.

"You know what?" he asks me.

"No, what?" I laugh.

"Your dad was right all those years ago."

"How so?" I ask Wes.

"He told me he knew what kind of man I was from the beginning and that I would always love you. He said that you and I would have what they had."

I look around the room filled with all of the people we love so much, and our home filled with love and happiness. "Because we do."

"Yes, we do," he tells me.

"Are you happy?" I ask him.

"Of course," Wes answers me. "This is the best day of my life."

What he hopefully knows by now, and I have done my very best to show him, is that every day with Wes has been the very best day of my life and each one is just a little better than the last.

the end

(For real this time. Mostly. Sort of.)

acknowledgements

Thank you! Thank you! Thank you!!!!

Thank you to the readers and bloggers who read *Tell Me a Story* and need to know how Claire's story played out. This book was for you. Thank you for loving her in spite of her flaws or for them and for wanting so badly to see her get her HEA. I hope you enjoyed watching her grow the way that I did and I hope you stick around to see where Lee finds himself in the future. You might just see some old friends pop in for visits. Special thank you to everyone who fell in love with the Dangerous Dames (Hey, girl!) and followed me over to the dark side. I promise next year is for you guys with *Dead and Gone, Layback, Dead and Deceived,* and *Hat Trick.*

Thank you to Nazarea Andrews at InkSlinger PR for being my hero. I couldn't do it without her. She runs a flawless event and put my little book baby out into the world in so many hands. I am so blessed to have her in my life. Also, huge thank you to Erin Fehres for running a wonderful Inkstagram tour. That was so much fun and she's a joy to work with.

Thank you to Stephanie Atienza for her love and support. She's a true friend and sister and I'm lucky to have her as my editor. She makes the crazy make sense and helped me flush out so much. I would be a mess without her. Thank you for being on this journey with me.

Thank you to Alyssa Garcia at Uplifting Designs

for such a gorgeous cover and formats. Thank you for making me see this series through to the end. It was a tough year and I'm better for it. Thank you for being on this journey with me.

Thank you to my mom and dad and granny who pass these books out to friends be they retired Marines or ladies at the beauty shop. Your support blows me away. Thank you so much for being my family. I'm lucky to have you.

And last, but never least, Thank you to my sweet husband, Sean. Thank you for always picking up the slack and for calling Alyssa to give me a hard time when I'm falling down on a deadline. Thank you for being an amazing husband and father. We are so lucky to have you. You inspire me every day. There are pieces of you in every hero and every HEA because you're the real deal. I'm forever grateful that you were at that party that night. The sound of motorcycle pipes will always mean fairytales to me. It was only ever you.

Better look out Dames, I'm coming for you!!!!

playlist

Wolves--Selena Gomez ft. Marshmelo
Stitches—Shawn Mendes
Dear Future Husband—Meghan Trainor
Criminal—Lindsay Ell
Say Something—Justin Timberlake featuring Chris Stapleton
Never Be the Same—Camila Cabello
Born to Love You—LANCO
Time's Up—The Song Suffragettes
Everything's Gonna Be Alright—David Lee Murphy & Kenny Chesney
Secrets—OneRepublic
Meant to Be—Florida Georgia Line featuring BeBe Rexha
Girls Like You—Maroon 5 featuring Cardi B.
Youngblood—5 Seconds of Summer
Cake by the Ocean—DNCE
1000 Years—Christina Perri

about the author

Jennifer is a thirty something lover of words, all words: the written, the spoken, the sung (even poorly), the sweet, the funny, and even the four letter variety. She is a native of San Diego, California where she grew up reading the Brownings and Rebecca with her mother and Clifford and the Dog who Glowed in the Dark with her dad, much to her mother's dismay.

Jennifer is a graduate of California State University San Marcos where she studied Criminology and Justice Studies. She is also a member of Alpha Xi Delta.

12 years ago, she was swept off her feet by her very own sailor. Today, they are happily married and the parents of a 9 year old and 8 year old twins. She lives in East Texas where she can often be found on the soccer fields, drawing with her children, or reading. Jennifer is convinced that if she puts her fitbit on one of the dogs, she might finally make her step goals. She loves a great romance, an alpha hero, and lots and lots of laughter.

stalk her

Website
JenniferRebeccaAuthor.com

Newsletter
JenniferRebeccaAuthor.com/Newsletter

Facebook
facebook.com/JenniferRebeccaAuthor

Twitter
@JenniRLreads

Instagram
@JenniRLreads

BookBub
bookbub.com/authors/jennifer-rebecca

Book+Main
bookandmainbites.com/users/22594

Dangerous Dames Facebook Group
facebook.com/groups/JRDangerousDames

also by jennifer rebecca

The Claire Goodnite Series
Tell Me a Story
Tuck Me in Tight
Say a Sweet Prayer
Kiss Me Goodnight

The Funerals and Obituaries Series
Dead and Buried
Dead and Gone, Coming Spring 2019
Dead and Deceived, Coming Late Summer 2019

The Murder on Ice Series
Attack Zone
Layback, Coming Summer 2019
Hat Trick, Coming Winter 2019

The Southern Heartbeats Series
Stand (Vol.1)
Joy (Vol.1.5)
Whiskey Lullabye (Vol.2)
Mercy (Vol.2.5), Free on Wattpad

hush little baby

a liam goodnite novel

Life in George Washington Township and the surrounding areas has once again been shaken up. Young, unwed mothers are turning up hacked to pieces after crude caesareans and their babies are nowhere to be found.

While overseeing the investigation, Captain Liam Goodnite receives some surprising news that just might give him the push that he needs to make the sexy Medical Examiner, Emma Parker, his once and for all.

Only Emma isn't one to forgive and forget.

Good thing life has taught Lee some tough lessons and now he's willing to do whatever it takes.

coming soon